I0530693

DEATH SQUAD: CITY POLICE

DOMINIC R. DANIELS & DOUG K. OWEN

COPYRIGHT©2015. Dominic R. Daniels & Doug K. Owen

ALL RIGHTS RESERVED.
ISBN: 0692402667
ISBN 13: 9780692402665

Dedicated to

Our Families and Friends

EXT. NEW YORK CITY - NIGHT (2095)

Open to the vast cyberpunk skyline of New York City, a decaying dystopian shell of a former majestic metropolis. Colossal monuments of a former empire faded deep in time. Yet advanced beyond in technological design what no mortal man could accomplish by his own hand of fate. Uptown some of the buildings are abandoned or on fire. Plumes of dense smoke are illuminated by police helicopter searchlights piercing through the pitch black clouds of darkness. At street level there are flashes of light and loud bangs. A gunfight is taking place down there.

EXT. STREETS - NIGHT

An armored police halftrack is speeding down the street in hot pursuit of a stolen military carrier truck (APC) carrying sectarian gang leaders. There are two police officers in the halftrack that are loading their weapons and contacting HQ. They are wearing regular body armor and helmets.

POLICE OFFICER
Central, this is Unit 672 in pursuit of sectarian leaders.
Suspects are armed and extremely dangerous. Do we
have a kill order?

                    HARTFORD (V.O.)
Negative. Pursue and capture.

                    POLICE OFFICER
       Central, copy -- AAH!

The APC opens the back hatch, and the gangsters are opening fire. They are armed with a heavy-duty minigun, and some of them have incendiary rounds. One of the police officers is ripped to bloody shreds right there in the cruiser as the bullets fly through the windshield and explosive rounds are popping all over the street. The driver of the police car swerves like crazy to avoid the fire.

                    POLICE OFFICER
     Jesus Christ! Officer down! Hartford! Give me a fuck-
     ing kill order, now!

                    HARTFORD (V.O.)
      Orders stand.

                    POLICE OFFICER
      You motherfucker!

Passing through an intersection, another vehicle pulls between the cop and the APC. It's an even bigger carrier than both of them, and there are gun turrets on the side and a large gun on the roof. It instantly opens fire on the APC.

                    POLICE OFFICER
      What the hell?

A searchlight illuminates the figure at the topmost gun turret. It's LOGAN KENNEDY, age 34. A wolfish convict member of the Executioner Squad, a psychopath with a wicked sense of humor and ultimate badass of a mutant. He's firing the heavy gun with a vengeance.

LOGAN
(on the officer's radio)
Back off porkbelly. This one's mine!

POLICE OFFICER
Aw, shit. It's them.

The large truck is waging a vicious battle against the APC. Bullets are flying between the two vehicles, and one of the gang leaders gets blasted in the APC, leaving a hefty bloodstain on the wall. In the large truck, one of the side windows opens and BISHOP CAIN, age 40, a buff African-American Special Forces Soldier and half human part cyborg emerges. The guy takes no shit, a warrior of the battlefield and of the streets. He fires a few rounds from a large rifle at the APC. MAX PRESCOTT, age mid-30's, sarcastic yet brave commanding leader, who is driving the truck.

MAX
Bishop, lay me down some cover fire!

BISHOP
Hang tight, son. I'm gonna smoke these mothers!

More gunfire, and Logan is relishing the battle, grinning like a madman as he fires the cannon indiscriminately.

LOGAN
Come on! You fuckers! Die motherfucker die!

Some bullets whiz past Logan and he ducks. Ooh, that was close. Logan picks up a communication device in the gun turret.

LOGAN
Hey honey, you got eyes on this?

JILL (V.O.)

Got 'em in my sight, ready to sweep.

LOGAN

Alright Jill, make it rain!

INT. COCKPIT - NIGHT

JILL. Age: Unknown. A sexy punk rock/goth mutant vampire and chopper pilot. An anarchist and mentally unstable with a thirst for bloodshed. She pops of the top of her joystick and pushes the big red button.

JILL

Rock and roll!

EXT. CHOPPER - NIGHT

Jill unleashes death supreme, shooting a missile that bursts into a cluster of mini missiles raining down utter destruction in a crimson inferno on the suspects' APC and leaving hefty craters in the street, sending them on a one-way ticket to hell.

LOGAN

Ah, I love cookouts!

Most of the squad is laughing at Logan's joke, all but Max. He frowns and hits the gas. The APC is now a bombed-out wreck, and two gang leaders, badly injured, partially burnt and unarmed, stumble out of the wreck. They hold their hands up in surrender, but the unyielding truck bears down on them and BAM! They are run right over and left as bloody messes on the pavement.

INT. SQUAD'S TRUCK - MOMENTS LATER

Inside the truck the Squad is relishing their latest victory. Logan fist-bumps with Bishop. Max is still driving, and he looks grumpy.

LOGAN

Hell yeah! Another one in the books, boys! It's gonna be vodka and sake bombs tonight!

BISHOP

And you're buying.

LOGAN

(growls and smiles)

Fine... asshole.

BISHOP

That's my job, wolf boy. Get used to it.

Logan grumbles and takes it in stride. In the driver's seat, Max turns on the comm.

MAX

Jill, you still up there?

INT. COCKPIT - NIGHT

JILL

Copy that. Situation is under control. We did good tonight.

MAX (V.O.)

I don't know about you guys but I'm not looking forward to later on.

JILL

Don't worry about it. I'll see you guys back at the station. I'm heading over now.

INT. SQUAD'S TRUCK - MOMENTS LATER

                    LOGAN
          What are you talking about? We're gonna get drunk
          and laid tonight!

                    MAX
          Not before Hartford tears us all some new assholes...
          <u>again</u>.

Instantly all the celebrating goes dead. They know what's coming, and it won't
be pretty.

EXT. POLICE HQ - NIGHT
Establishing shot of Police HQ exterior. It's an old run-down fire station with a
large shutter door up front. Most of the station's actual workings are in the base-
ment's levels. The topmost levels are basic offices.

INT. POLICE HQ - NIGHT
Establishing shot of the police station lobby. Human and alien cops have their
hands full with tapping information on computers or dealing with suspects, including strung-out crackheads and flirty prostitutes. One of the cons pulls a
knife and the cops beat him to an inch of his life. He looks not too different
from the roadkill from earlier.

    The Squad members walk through the crowds, still in uniform. The cops
look at them with a mix of admiration and pity. The assorted scum are almost
terrified. Instantly the place goes silent.

                    MAX
                (looking around)
          What? Aren't you glad to see us?

POLICE CLERK
Uh, you guys kinda fried those rat bastards uptown.

LOGAN
So what? I thought you guys were used to that by now.
What's the problem?

POLICE CLERK
Not those suckers. We needed them alive. You blew it
on this one.

Max lets out a sigh of regret. He's trying to brace himself.

BISHOP
Aw, crap.

POLICE CLERK
Anyway, the dictator is in his office, and he's really
pissed. Watch yourselves.

As the Squad walks to an elevator, one of the other cops starts whistling
"Taps."

BISHOP
Shut up, Davis.

DAVIS
Sorry. Hey Bishop, good luck in there man.

BISHOP
Thanks.

INT. HARTFORD'S OFFICE - NIGHT

The office is rather large, but still cluttered with paperwork. HARTFORD, age 50's, himself is bald, hairy, fat and his face is a deep red and twisted in a perpetual state of rage. A true asshole who is always uptight and dictatorial just like Hitler. He's fuming mad when the Squad members enter, Max, Bishop, Logan and Jill.

> HARTFORD
>
> You sloppy goddamn stupid assholes! Do you realize what you've just done, all the damage you've caused? I got the mayor breathing down my neck and you've just cost the city millions of dollars! I should pull the fucking trigger and kill all you worthless pieces of shit!

> MAX
>
> Be doing us all a favor.

> BISHOP
>
> Hey Prescott, shut up. I got a family to get back to someday. And I want to be alive for that.

> HARTFORD
> (slamming on his desk)
>
> <u>Shut up!</u>

They all stand at (somewhat) attention. Hartford takes some pills for his heart condition and draws a deep breath.

> HARTFORD
>
> Those suspects you killed out there, they had intel on the Phalanx resistance group. They would've told us everything about their plans! Now thanks to you all we got nothing! We're back to square one!

LOGAN

Those guys took out one of your own back there. We saved the other guy. I think you owe us for that at least.

HARTFORD

I don't owe you a damn thing! You owe <u>me</u> some gratitude for not killing you right where you stand!

JILL

You could've at least told us you wanted them alive.

HARTFORD

<u>I did!</u> But you didn't listen to me! You <u>never</u> listen to me!

MAX

Easy, chief...

Hartford downs some more pills.

HARTFORD

The only thing that doesn't stop me from doing you all in is the damn board's decision. You all have a hearing tomorrow at 9AM. If you're even a second late or throw some sass I'll have you on Death Row immediately!

BISHOP

Like you could do anything else to us.

HARTFORD

<u>Get out!</u>

INT. GPE BOARDROOM - MORNING

The Boardroom is nice and spacious. Metal paneling on the walls and a large window that looks out to the city. In front of it with their backs to the window are the Review Board sitting along a large, long podium that is some ten feet above the floor, looking down at the Squad members, who are kept in shackles. Several officers have guns trained on each of them. The Board members all middle-aged, stare down at each of the Squad members and tap something on their computers.

> MR. GOLDSTEIN
> It is the purpose of this board meeting to examine and review the case record files of Executioner Squad Zero-Two-Five-Seven, and to determine if the members are worthy to re-enter civilized society after completion of your tour of duty. Please step forward when your name is called.

> JILL
> (through clenched teeth)
> Here it comes, more bureaucratic shit.

> MR. GOLDSTEIN
> No talking!

Some officers ready their weapons at Jill.

> MR. LYLESBERG
> Max Prescott, step forward.

Max takes a step forward.

> MR. LYLESBERG
> Max Prescott, Age 36. Human White Male, arrested for manslaughter by killing 100 people, aliens and humans

in a bomb squad case. Sentence: 30 years Rehabilitation or Execution.

MAX

It was an accident.

MR. GOLDSTEIN

You've already had your trial, Mr. Prescott! Be silent for the proceedings!

MR. LYLESBERG

Former SWAT officer and decorated commander, now appointed team leader of Executioner Squad 0257. Recent missions include urban pacification, apprehending known affiliates with the Phalanx group and other syndicates. However, Chief Hartford notes an extreme tendency to disregard procedure and public endangerment. Probation denied.

Max groans.

MR. GOLDSTEIN

Bishop Cain.

Bishop steps up.

MR. LYLESBERG

Bishop Cain, Age 40. Human with cybernetic implants, African-American Male, arrested for armed robbery, multiple gang vigilante killings and drug smuggling. Sentence: 20 years Rehabilitation or Execution.

BISHOP

Correct, sir.

MR. O'DONNELL

Designated second in command of Executioner Squad 0257. Former Special Forces soldier, served in China, Korea, and Guatemala. Service in the Squad marked with insubordination to the team leader and to Chief Hartford, as well as extreme depression and suicidal tendencies. Dangerous and reckless behavior. Probation denied.

Bishop holds his head down.

MR. GOLDSTEIN

Jill Morgan.

Jill scowls at the Board.

JILL

What do you want?

MR. GOLDSTEIN

Please step forward, Ms. Morgan.

She does so.

MR. O'DONNELL

Jill Morgan, age: Unknown. Mutant, White female. Arrested for illegal weapons smuggling and aggravated murder of an officer in cold blood.

Sentence: 20 Rehabilitation or Execution.

MR. LYLESBERG

Former Air Force helicopter pilot, designated pilot and air support for Executioner Squad 0257. Record marked with property damage, loss of civilian lives, and grand larceny of government property. Noted manic depressive and bipolar disorder, and recently attributed to several cases of assault and attempted murder during off-duty hours. Probation denied.

JILL

Hey, those guys were willing donors! That's not my fault.

MR. GOLDSTEIN

That is irrelevant to this hearing! Step back!

Jill steps back, grumbling.

MR. GOLDSTEIN

Logan Kennedy.

Logan steps up with an evil smile. The Board members are terrified. Good thing he's kept in heavy chains that are laced with silver.

LOGAN

You had to put silver in these cuffs, didn't you? These things hurt like hell!

MR. O'DONNELL

Logan Kennedy, age: 34. Former human turned Mutant, white male. Arrested for various serial killings of 55 people. Sentence: 40 years Rehabilitation or Execution.

LOGAN

(sarcastic and angry)

I did not ask to be a mutant. I was turned into one by accident! Courtesy of my former boss for a bad debt.

Excuse me if I don't have a psychotic episode now and
then.

A beat.

                    MR. LYLESBERG
If you please. Mr. Kennedy.

Logan shuts up looking bilious.

                    MR. LYLESBERG
Formerly involved in underground fighting circuits and
professional prizefighting. Banned from the sport for killing an opponent, and found associating with organized
crime elements as an assassin for hire. Record is marked
with extreme aggression and reckless abandon for civilian
lives. Extremely unstable and violent. Probation denied.

                    LOGAN
You want violent? How about I rip your face off?

                    MR. GOLDSTEIN
Mr. Kennedy, you should be aware that the officers in
this room are using ammunition laced with silver.

Logan calms down.

                    MR. GOLDSTEIN
That's better. It is the findings of this board that all members of the squad are ineligible for probation at this time.
                    (beat)
However, your past successful missions have brought
a large reduction among the criminal element in the

city. For that the board is willing to be generous. You will be re-assigned to Chief Hartford for one last mission. If you are successful, you may be reconsidered for the reduction of your sentences and if possible an earlier release. However, if insubordination occurs again, failure will be met with rescinding active duty and immediate execution by firing squad. This concludes the hearing. Next review for surviving Squad members will be in six months.

MAX

"Surviving Squad members?" Thanks for the vote of confidence.

MR. O'DONNELL

...We hope. Mr. Prescott as team leader you will report to Dr. Cornelius Cedrick in R&D for briefing today at 3PM. The rest of you will join him later when assigned. Good day gentlemen and lady present.

INT. HALLS OUTSIDE BOARDROOM - MORNING

The Squad members still have their chains on, and being led away at gunpoint back to a processing room where their chains will be taken off. Soon they will be heading out to kill some time.

MAX

Well, that went well.

JILL

Speak for yourself. We put our asses on the line and they still don't cut any breaks. I'm gonna slash their throats next chance I get.

                            BISHOP
If we ever want to get out of this alive, you wouldn't.
You want to get us in more trouble?

                            LOGAN
She's got a point. Dead here or dead on the streets,
we're screwed either way.

                            BISHOP
Shut up Logan. We're gonna get out of this and live.
Grow up.

The Squad members leave the building in their truck, bound for the police station to receive their latest assignment. Meanwhile...

INT. GPE BOARDROOM - MORNING
This Boardroom is on the 150th floor of the Empire State Building; GPE bought the building long ago, as well as the entire city. GPE, Global Placement Enterprises, runs such endeavors as military technology, transportation, colonization of space, and government/diplomacy/peacekeeping. This includes the Executioner Squad program.

ROBERT HESSMAN, age 52, enters the Boardroom late. He is half human and half Akaritan alien. His features are humanoid with some Akaritan features. The rest of the board, which is comprised of more Akaritan than human members, looks at HESSMAN when he walks in. He takes a seat next to SNYDER, a human.

                            HESSMAN
Did I miss anything?

                            SNYDER
No, just the opening quarterly statements.

The company's director, an Akaritan named GENE WESLEY, age 50, stares at Hessman and Snyder.

GENE

Well, now that our friend Mr. Hessman has seen fit to join us, perhaps we can discuss the matter of Project Chimara finally.

That name sends a ripple through the room.

GENE

Mr. Hessman, you as a first-generation hybrid understand better than most the struggles we face daily.

Gene gets up from his chair and walks near Hessman.

GENE

Ever since the first of the Akaritan landed over fifty years ago, we have tried to earn a place within the realm of human society. The planet was already burdened with a massive human population and lack of resources, and our arrival was neither expected nor welcomed. To this very day there is still the threat of war looming over all our people.

SNYDER

Yeah, that probably would happen ever since you people did what you did.

GENE

I beg your pardon, Mr. Snyder?

SNYDER

You came here to our planet and you weaseled your
way into our governments and our lives. Ever since
then the whole place has gone to hell. You didn't "earn"
your place, you stole it!

Some board members, all of them Akaritan, don't take too kindly to that state-
ment and start shouting at him. Hessman tries to steady him.

HESSMAN

Watch it Lawrence.

SNYDER

What? It's true! Ever since they arrived, you couldn't
walk two blocks without some humans and aliens bickering at each other, and now we have, what do you call
it? A police state? Total breakdown of society?

GENE

We need not be reminded about that, Mr. Snyder. We
have enough problems as it is with humans still being
uncomfortable with us.

SNYDER

That's a nice choice of words.

GENE

(turning to Hessman)

Mr. Hessman, we at GPE have held to the belief that
the world deserves better, and it is only with the willing participation of the best minds from Earth and the
Akaritan working together for the greater good. For
advancement, for peace, for the good of all people.

And your Project Chimara has been an embarrassment to this entire company!

HESSMAN

With respect, sir and members of the board, that was the goal of Project Chimara all along: advancement. The idea behind the project was to re-map the human genome to a higher state. All those incidents, those mutations, were part of the procedure.

GENE

Effectively creating a new species, as it were, one that was also unwelcome on the planet.

Hessman is on the defensive.

HESSMAN

Not at all, but a more evolved form of a human being. I started the project to bring advancement to the people. Greater abilities, greater potential! However, thanks to the mutants' uprising around the country, the damned government instigated species cleansing!

GENE

Cleansing?

HESSMAN

You know what I mean! Death camps, and the Executioner Squad program. I know this is all being laid at my feet, but what happened with the mutants was no fault of mine, or anyone in this company! They simply didn't fit in with society. Why else would they resort to violence?

SNYDER

The mutants were facing discrimination, just like every other Akaritan out there. They just took it a bit too far is all.

GENE

Be that as it may...

HESSMAN
(interrupting)
We all had good intentions.

GENE
(staring angrily at Hessman)
This board is highly unsatisfied with your project. The mutants are still in the general population, and they have come under extreme scrutiny from the press and the government. The mutants, we believe, are possible carriers of the plague that has recently struck the city and its people, human and Akaritan.

HESSMAN

What?! You're accusing them of causing the plague? That's preposterous!

GENE

We're calling an investigation into all of Project Chimara, to protect the interest of this company as well as our stockholders.

HESSMAN
(catching his breath)
Mr. Welsey, gentlemen of the board, I can assure you that Project Chimara was started with the best of

intentions and well within the company's philosophy of advancement for all. I can also be quite sure that the plague has nothing to do with the mutants.

SNYDER

Robert is correct about our findings Mr. Wesley. To help keep the public calm we have coordinated with local law enforcement and The Inter-Species Rehabilitation Agency to send investigation squad teams to seek the source of these outbreaks. It is our belief that this plague was not caused by the mutant population, but that someone created it and began spreading it. In other words, sectarian terrorists.

BILL RICHARDSON, age 49, a fellow vice-chairman, speaks.

RICHARDSON

Due to the recent attacks on the city from the rebel organization known as Phalanx, we could agree with you on that Mr. Snyder. However, we do not know for certain that it was them. But we need to focus upon fixing the problems that Project Chimara has caused for us.

GENE

Bearing in mind of course that Dr. Walton has disappeared some time ago. His role has been very difficult to fill, and he hasn't made himself easy to find either. We need to find him.

HESSMAN

I've already been trying to track him down. I've had every private investigator from here to Jersey on the case, but we have nothing.

SNYDER

Is he dead?

HESSMAN

No.

RICHARDSON

In that case, Dr. Pike would be perfect for this research project to replace Dr. Walton. His expertise would make him ideal to pick up the reins of Chimara until Dr. Walton can be found.

HESSMAN

He is right. Dr. Pike is the best scientist we have at GPE. I also fully endorse him for this project. He has proven to achieve results in all our research endeavors.

DR. HERBERT PIKE, AGE 34. Alien Scientist. Formerly Dr. Cornelius' assistant, high altruistic and noble, now lead scientist in GPE biological department and also fellow executive board member, speaks.

DR. PIKE

(to Richardson and Hessman)

Thank you gentlemen. I appreciate your vote of support. I will get in contact with Dr. Cedrick to begin research on synthesizing a cure.

A beat.

HESSMAN

Are you sure that is a smart move to make, Herbert? You do understand that the man you speak of is guilty of treason against the state and a known former terrorist himself who killed 1,000 workers in one of our weapons plants.

DR. PIKE

Sir, he is a brilliant scientist. He has studied every possible virus and dread disease known to man. He is an expert in the field as a master biochemist and geneticist. If anyone would be able to help us solve this plague dilemma, he would be a perfect fit. He is currently being held under close watch as a lead scientist for ISRA and has with his rehabilitation in the state's program, proven to be no longer a danger to city or the general public.

GENE

How can we be sure, that Cedrick will cooperate with us?

DR. PIKE

He will on this matter. He trusts me. During his reform, he has created many cures for certain diseases and has saved the lives of countless people, both Akaritan and human. He is no longer the man we once knew as a vile terrorist but an ambassador of the common good for the state.

The board murmurs among themselves about this.

GENE

Very well. See to it.

DR. PIKE

Yes sir.

GENE

That is all for these proceedings. Good day gentlemen.

The board rises and leaves the room.

INT. HALLS OUTSIDE BOARDROOM - MORNING

Dr. Pike and Hessman speak on their way out and head into a crystal clear glass shaft elevator going down to the lower floors.

DR. PIKE

Thank you Robert for your support. I am eager for this assignment.

HESSMAN

Not a problem Herbert. You are an excellent scientist. Without your support Chimera would not have reached the depths we know today of the human genome and its metamorphic abilities. You make me proud.

DR. PIKE

Thank you sir. I only hope that I can make this project successful as the others.

HESSMAN

You will. Trust me.

DR. PIKE

When do you want to me contact Cedrick?

HESSMAN

Immediately.

INT. POLICE HQ - R&D LAB - MORNING

Max Prescott is down in R&D to report to DR. CEDRICK, age mid-40's. A poised man and intelligent alien with a dry sense of humor, Cedrick is busy typing on his LCD Projection Computer system that is bigger than Andre the Giant about a chemical compound report in conjunction with a drug bust case.

MAX

(joking)

Hey Doc. How is life down in the pit, with the rats?

DOC CEDRICK

(sarcastic)

Roaches or rats. What the difference. I'm in hell.

MAX

At least you got the less dangerous jobs. I envy you.

DOC CEDRICK

(sarcastic)

Envy you say. I would rather bathe in the living bodily fluids of a Laraxian beast's nether regions, than be stuck here to rot.

MAX

(joking)

I think I'd take the Laraxian.

DOC CEDRICK

I take it Hartford sent you down here. What's that walking, bloated tub of bile want this time?

MAX

Beats me, but it looks like the last grand hoorah. If we don't nail this assignment I can kiss my ass and my pension goodbye.

DOC CEDRICK
(dry)

Hence, the joke to ease the pain. I feel yours with ease.

MAX

Ha ha.

Dr. Cedrick just smirks.

Dr. Cedrick receives a phone call via comm device.

DOC CEDRICK

Hold up a second.

Doc answers the phone.

DOC CEDRICK

R&D. Dr. Cedrick speaking.

A beat.

DOC CEDRICK

Yes sir... ugh huh.

A beat.

DOC CEDRICK

Please holograph the report to me. I will have the file pulled up in a second.

A beat.

> DOC CEDRICK
>
> Thank you sir. Yes... Officer Prescott just arrived. I will notify him immediately.

A beat.

> DOC CEDRICK
>
> Thank you sir.

Dr. Cedrick hangs up his comm device.

> MAX
>
> So what's the deal? Hartford raising hell?

> DOC CEDRICK
>
> More like hell is raising him. He is fired up about the boards review. I think he wanted to put us all out of our misery sooner than we wanted.

> MAX
>
> Figures.

Dr. Cedrick draws up the holograph file and shows the hologram images as he explains the next mission.

> DOC CEDRICK
>
> Anyway. Here is the report.

Just then the rest of the team comes in, Bishop, Jill and Logan present.

> MAX
>
> Oh nice. You chowder heads finally showed up.

LOGAN
(joking)
Hey, Prescott. At least I can get it up.

MAX
(laughs)
Wise ass.

Dr. Cedrick brings up the holograph report on the main computer console. The projector shoots out of beam of light with a display of images.

DOC CEDRICK
Here's the deal. For this mission the objective is to seek out the ones who created this plague and stop them at any cost.

JILL
What do you mean Doc? I thought the city was the one to give all mutants a bad rap. Why should we help them? They thought we were the cause with all the rumors in the news.

DOC CEDRICK
Because our asses are on the line. Besides. They were wrong -- observe.

Dr. Cedrick pulls up the hologram image of a operation autopsy of dead mutant and Akaritan. These are dead plague victims' corpses.

DOC CEDRICK
Two cadaver corpses to the demon of the 8th power. Mega zits and pus shooter city, on their faces that is. These poor bastards had their blood vessels in their

bodies explode before they died. Their faces were melted, like being hit with battery acid. Their skin looks like if it was peeled back like a banana.

JILL

Yikes.

BISHOP

You got to be kidding me. This plague is bad, but that looks worse than a smack head with AIDS on Sunday.

DOC CEDRICK

I concur.

MAX

When these guys come in?

DOC CEDRICK

Two hours ago. My former colleague Dr. Pike informed Hartford who then told me. The departed came into Midtown at Saint Agatha's Hospital of Hope around 1PM. We got a blood sample from both of the corpses here.

MAX

So?

DOC CEDRICK

So the results found in the bloodwork revealed that these two individuals died with a powerful drug in their systems.

JILL

What the difference? Smack heads end up dead in the street like these all the time.

DOC CEDRICK

Not like these. Look at this.

Dr. Cedrick pulls up more images on the screen of the blood cells.

DOC CEDRICK

The molecular structure in these blood cells is highly unstable. Revealing traces of two different compounds. And it definitely has deadly side effects. Mescalinthropine-Eskalondor. A powerful Akaritan synthetic drug. Popular on the black market. Look.

Just then they see the blood cells explode blowing up the neutron microscope and the camera with it the video feed goes to snow.

MAX

Christ!

DOC CEDRICK

Not quite. But after the incident occurred, they managed to capture a live one... well, barely, anyway. He is a human with the same aliment in the blood.

The group continues to watch the hologram feed of the live captive. The live captive is festering all over the place showing similar features as the dead corpses. Going insane tearing out his skin that is burning in agonizing pain. Screaming like a madman back from hell ready to head back and burn.

LOGAN

How come we did not see this before on the street?

DOC CEDRICK

Whoever is creating these drugs must be making new variations. But also has been mixed with something else, a biological hormone that is mixed in. The suspect we received down in containment was under lockdown. He literally showed the same symptoms of the cadavers just before he died. They had this extra compound in their systems as also. Someone in the city not only created this virus but is supplying it also. We need to find out who and what their operation is before it spreads further.

JILL

What do you mean we?

DOC CEDRICK

Oh Hartford didn't tell you? I have been assigned to join you on this mission. Not in combat but on side for backup support in the lab.

MAX

Is this a capture or kill mission?

DOC CEDRICK

Capture. Killing, though, might be a good idea. But I doubt Hartford will agree with that notion. What does it matter anyway? Miranda rights no longer exist. Your job is find the criminals and arrest or kill them. With the exception to those who can pass a psychic halo collar test to prove their innocence.

BISHOP
Where do you think they got this hormone at?

DOC CEDRICK
Government labs I suppose. Someone could have broken into them and stolen the necessary materials. The point is we got to stop it or the entire city will be soon become infected.

MAX
Any other info?

DOC CEDRICK
Yes, other symptoms of users... when this virus is in the system, they show signs of physical deformity that occur inside and out of the body including a complete mental breakdown of the mind exhibiting complete psychotic features. To put it bluntly -- a walking madman.

JILL
Where do we start to look? This city is big and large in size.

LOGAN
(jokes crazy)
Just like your tits.

JILL
You're such a furrie, always horny.

LOGAN
(smiling)

Hey what'd I say?

BISHOP

Enough jokes, let's get going. We got a lot of ground
to cover.

MAX

It might be good to check out the organized crime syndicates, they got more power to push drugs than any of
the street gangs here in the city.

LOGAN

That's a good idea.

MAX

I'll get in touch with Amber. She can crack into the
systems to see what we can find. A lot of the syndicates are at war right now. Killings are through the
roof. It's as if the streets are running red with blood
every day.

BISHOP

Be careful about Hartford. Amber is his pride and joy
as Daddy's little girl. You get her involved in this with
us and he'll have our status revoked. We'll be stepping
one foot closer in the grave.

INT. ARCHIVES ROOM - EVENING

The Archives Room is filled with filing cabinets for cases that haven't been trans-
ferred digitally yet. Against the far wall past the narrow rows of cabinets is a wide

open space with a massive LED screen and console taking up the wall. Max squeezes his way through the narrow rows and into this open space (and heaving a sigh of relief) and walks over to the girl at the console. Her back is turned to him.

MAX

Got a minute, Babydoll?

The girl turns around to reveal an extremely beautiful face and body. She is AMBER HARTFORD, the Chief's daughter mid 30's. She works in Archives and she and Max tend to flirt with each other.

AMBER HARTFORD

Hey handsome. What do you need down here?

MAX

Info. The usual deal.

AMBER HARTFORD

Something special in mind?

MAX

I wish.

AMBER HARTFORD

What does that mean?

MAX

I wish I could get between those lovely legs of yours. Of course, Daddy wouldn't like that.

AMBER HARTFORD

Daddy doesn't like anything. So what's the case you need?

MAX

I need to do a cross-reference check against any of the local syndicates. I need anything that has to do with drug or weapon smuggling. It's about the plague that's got the whole town turning into rot.

AMBER HARTFORD

Well, there's only a couple thousand syndicate members in the New York area. Where do you want me to start?

MAX

How about the most recent drug bust on record?

Amber taps some info into the console and brings up on screen the dossier on the weapons dealer Name, face, recent charges, and other information appear.

AMBER HARTFORD

Leonard Murdo, Code-name "Abaddon." He's a trafficker of illegal arms and stolen Akaritan tech. His organization is wanted for at least 250 known murders and killing 22 regular cops and at least five members of other death squads.

MAX

Oh yeah, him. All we got was half of his private army. I'd love to finally settle it with him.

AMBER HARTFORD

Good luck on that, Prescott. I'll keep looking and see if there's anything to tie him with the virus.

MAX

He'll know something. I'll get back to you in a few.

INT. HARTFORD'S OFFICE - EVENING

Max steps into the office, to find the other DS members, Logan, Bishop, Jill and even DOC hunched against the right wall. Bishop is nursing a wound on the back of his neck.

>   BISHOP
>   Ow... shit.

Max looks around confused. Hartford is at his desk with a large metallic gun. He's reloading it and aiming it at Max.

>   MAX
>   (confused)
>   Did I miss something?

>   HARTFORD
>   (stern)
>   Turn around... now.

>   MAX
>   How about no?

>   HARTFORD
>   Fine, then let's do it the hard way. Officers!

Two Officers enter the room. Hartford nods at them.

>   HARTFORD
>   Grab him!

The Officers grab Max by the arms. There is a small struggle. One of them aims a gun at the other DS members to keep them against the wall.

MAX

The hell? What is this?

The Officers turn him around to face the door. Behind him, Hartford aims the large gun and shoots him in the back of the neck. Max screams in pain. The Officers release him and they exit. Max is kneeling on the ground, holding the back of his neck. There's a small crater there, and it hurts like all get out.

HARTFORD

It's a tracking device. Board's making it mandatory for all squad members.

MAX

You're full of shit.

HARTFORD

You even touch that device and it'll send a poison through your whole system right to your brain. You'll be dead in ten seconds. Make the plague look like a nosebleed.

MAX

Hey Chief, seriously, when we get outta this, I'm gonna kick your ass.

HARTFORD

The hell you will. Suit up and get ready for a mission. Briefing's in an hour. Now get out.

INT. POLICE HQ LANDING BAY - EVENING

The DS members are fully suited up and loading weapons and ammo into a large APC, a personnel carrier jet. Bishop is carrying smaller magazines while Logan hauls a massive minigun.

BISHOP

Get the lead out, Wolfie. Not getting paid by the hour!

LOGAN

Fuck you, we're not even getting paid at all.

MAX

Cut the crap guys. Load up.

Max's comm rings, and he answers it.

MAX

Prescott.

DOC CEDRICK (V.O.)

Officer Prescott, I've been assigned as support and tac-tics advisor. I've been switched over and moved to your squad.

MAX

Great, just what we need. A fucking Einstein.

DOC CEDRICK (V.O.)

I'm not a physicist, officer. I'm a geneticist. I'm on my way to join you in the landing bay. I need to collect more viral samples from the field.

MAX

Fine. Get your scaly ass up here. We're shipping out in ten.

Amber taps Max on the shoulder as he hangs up. Max spins around looking like he's about to bitch-slap someone, then puts his hand down.

MAX

Don't do that!

AMBER HARTFORD

Whatever. Listen, I got the info on your next run.
Looks like it's Murdo tonight.

MAX

Abaddon again? Great. Where's he hiding?

AMBER HARTFORD

Down at the warehouse district. Shipping yards. He's
meeting with some types who have been tied to the
viral spill. Probably another syndicate, and he's selling
a lot of weapons and stuff to them.

MAX

Let me guess, stop the deal and kill everyone, right?

AMBER HARTFORD

Not this time, we need Abaddon alive. He knows
something about who let the virus out. We need him
and as many others of his crew as we can get.

MAX

(a beat)

Alright.

Max turns to go into the APC, but amber grabs his arm.

AMBER HARTFORD

Max, if anything happens, like that thing on the streets
last week, well, I don't know if my dad is going to let it go.

MAX

Don't worry. For you, we'll play by the rules. Just don't
expect it twice.

Amber turns around as Max boards the jet. She comes face-to-face with Doc
Cedrick. She screams a bit.

DOC CEDRICK

My apologies, Miss Hartford. I'm late for the team's
departure.

AMBER HARTFORD

Sorry, I'm still not used to seeing... well, you guys.

DOC CEDRICK

Akaritan?

AMBER HARTFORD

Yeah. Well, good luck you guys.

DOC CEDRICK

Ma'am.

Doc boards the jet and it takes off. It is a large, hulking aircraft with a vertical
takeoff/landing system designed for troop transport. It does have a few armor
plates and guns on the hull.

INT. ARMORED PERSONNEL CARRIER - NIGHT

The DS members are seated against the walls of the transport. Logan is clutch-
ing a rifle that is several times larger than he is.

LOGAN

So what's the game?

MAX

Abaddon. He was the arms dealer that got away last time. Remember him?

LOGAN
(gets excited)
Yeah, still can't believe he got away when we had him cornered downtown. I'm gonna rip his throat out.

JILL

Me first!

MAX

Cool it! Not this time. The higher-ups need him alive. They think he knows something about who spilled the virus all over town.

Jill crosses her arms.

JILL

Hate it when they say that.

DOC CEDRICK

Miss Morgan, you should know that the virus is easily transmitted through fluid contact. If you intend to quench your thirst on contaminated blood, it'll be your last meal.

JILL
(sarcastically)
Immortal says hi.

The APC jumps a bit, and everyone is shaken in their seats. Logan wasn't strapped in, and he bounces out of his seat and clatters to the floor.

LOGAN

Goddamnit Bishop!

EXT. NEW YORK CITY - NIGHT

The APC levels itself back out and soars over the city. Scrolling down, we go from the skies to street level, where the population of NYC is going about their business on the streets. We see human, mutant and Akaritan people together in the crowds going in and out of small shops and large hotels. In the slums there are even Akaritan and mutant call-girls with voracious bodies. A human is checking out the non-human merchandise on display with a horny look.

HORNY GUY

Mmm, oh yeah, get some exotic tail!

Over in the business district, the Stock Exchange is filled with human and Akaritan investors dressed in fine suits and reading the Daily Street Journal (cover story, GPE's stock declines in wake of mutant outbreak).

EXT. SLUMS - NIGHT

Outside a small run-down diner, a small gang of humans is cornering two Akaritans.

HUMAN #1

We don't want your kind here!

HUMAN #2

Get the fuck off our planet, scale-head!

The Akaritans are deeply offended, and try to defend themselves against one of the humans who has started shoving them against a wall.

AKARITAN #1

What did we do to you?

HUMAN #2

You moved here! Shoved us all onto the streets!

HUMAN #1

Let's rip these fuckers apart and see if they bleed!

The humans and Akaritans get into a huge fistfight. One Akaritan lands a solid blow against a human's face, and another human retaliates by stabbing him with a switchblade. An Akaritan is cornered by a human with a huge handgun.

HUMAN #2

Humans forever! Hail Phalanx!

He shoots one Akaritan. Blue-green swirls of alien blood paint the walls. The other Akaritan closes his eyes and holds two fingers to his head, then points them at him like gun-fingers. Instantly, the gunman's head starts pulsating.

HUMAN #2

(shouting)

Aaah! What the fuck!

The human clutches his head madly while the Akaritan keeps his gaze centered on his prey. The human's head starts to throb and contort, as if something is squirming beneath his skin, ready to pop. A beam of light comes from the Akaritan's forehead and a massive invisible force erupts from the alien's fingers and the human's head explodes in a crimson burst. Three police officers, one of them Akaritan, arrive on the scene with guns drawn at the surviving Akaritan victim.

POLICE OFFICER HUMAN

Freeze! Hands on your head!

The Akaritan does so as the police look around at the bodies. They look ready to kill him.

> AKARITAN #1
>
> It was self-defense officer!

The Akaritan officer closes his eyes to read his mind.

> POLICE OFFICER AKARITAN
>
> He's right. Self-defense. Let him go.

As the officers pull away, the Akaritan stares at one of the human bodies.

> AKARITAN #1
>
> Your planet? Not when he's done with you primitives.

EXT. SHIPPING YARD - NIGHT

The APC hovers over a large shipping yard. Steel containers form a maze that leads to a cluster of warehouses. Lights are on at the warehouse, but there's not enough room for the APC to land safely near there. The APC lands on the far side of the container maze.

> JILL
>
> (over the sound of engines)
>
> Game time, boys! Time to play!

The squad members arm themselves, including Doc Cedrick, who holds a large machine gun. Bishop looks at him like he told a bad joke.

> BISHOP
>
> Really?

                    DOC CEDRICK
        Quite.

He cocks the gun.

    Max leads the team in a tight formation through the shipping yard. They follow in a tight line one by one. Bishop and Logan point their guns in every direction looking for snipers or security cameras. Doc looks a bit nervous and uncomfortable holding a human-made gun.

                    DOC CEDRICK
        Micro-projectile weapons? You humans could do much
        better.

                    LOGAN
        Well, that's what we got you scaleheads for!

                    DOC CEDRICK
                    (offended)
        Watch it.

The maze is dark save only for the glow of the squad's flashlights and weapons. Out of the maze and into the glow of overhead lights. Ahead at the warehouse, a group of people are gathering. They are in silhouette, but they are armed.

INT. WAREHOUSE - NIGHT

Inside the warehouse, ABADDON is surrounded by goons about to close a deal with a group of Akaritan and half-breed buyers. Abaddon is Middle-Eastern/European mix, with a short beard and a trench coat. In front of him are several wooden crates, each one filled with stolen Akaritan weapons and other miscellaneous tech.

ABADDON

As promised, gentlemen, right on schedule. The latest
and most advanced in alien weaponry. Laser-guided,
pulse-fire rifles that can split atoms. Bio-rifles that
draw off human energy to fire concentrated bursts. It'll
never need to reload as long as you are holding it.

The Akaritan clients are not amused.

AKARITAN CLIENT #1

We know what it is, human. We built it.

ABADDON

Beg your pardon sir. I am just informing the other buyers who are not, shall we say, related to you.

AKARITAN CLIENT #2

These wares were stolen from the first Akaritan set-
tlers fifty years ago. You're selling us antique junk.

ABADDON

You're much mistaken. I have taken the liberty of
adding some repairs and modifications. I've studied
Akaritan tech for several years; I could almost make
a pulse rifle using balsa wood and a chemistry set. If
your people need weapons, then I'm always glad to do
business with you.

One Akaritan opens a crate and withdraws a small silvery handgun, Akaritan-
type. He crushes it with one hand like a soda can.

ABADDON

Well, I also offer a warranty as well.

AKARITAN CLIENT 2

I don't think so. No human being is capable of replicat-
ing our technology, and we will not entrust our might
to a primitive mind who still scrawls on scraps of paper
to get messages across.

The Akaritan throws the crushed gun to the ground. Its innards are rusted and dead.

AKARITAN CLIENT #1

You're selling us outdated and useless merchandise.
Swindler!

The Akaritans draw (better) guns at the humans, who draw their own brand of
guns. It's a Mexican standoff with Abaddon in the middle.

ABADDON

I assure you, my weapons are the finest quality, and my
modifications will ensure constant operation. If you
would like a demonstration...

The cargo door on the far side of the room bursts open in an explosion, and the
DS members start entering.

ABADDON

Well, speak of the devil. How about that demonstration? Open fire!

Abaddon's gang tries to open fire, but the DS is quicker on the draw. They fire
first and Abaddon and some of his goons take cover behind some crates and
tables. They try to return fire, but their weapons aren't working.

ABADDON GOON #1

Shit! They don't work!

The DS is laying waste to Abaddon's goons and the other Akaritans. Max is looking determined and stoic, Bishop grits his teeth and wants it all to be over. Jill and Logan are reveling in the bloodshed. Doc, however, treats the gun like something ugly and looks cold and emotionless, numb to death. Some of the Akaritans fight back with pulse-rifles that shoot bursts of glowing energy at the squad, but the squad uses cover like experts and dispatch them easily in gooey bursts. By the end of the battle, there are red, blue and green bloodstains everywhere, as if a painter went insane. Only Abaddon and three goons survive, but two of the goons are heavily wounded.

MAX

Report! Everyone alright?

BISHOP

All clear!

LOGAN

Son of a bitch, shit...

MAX

Logan, you with us?

LOGAN

I hate cleanup jobs.

JILL

I'm still here.

A straggler tries to crawl away from the bodies. Jill grabs him and bites his throat out. Blood flies through the sky and Jill drinks deeply from his body like juice, and she's really thirsty with blood on her face. She feels ecstasy from feeding and then drops the body and wipes her face with a white handkerchief. Abaddon looks on from behind a table with a terrified look.

JILL

Mmmmm... yummy.

Abaddon is completely petrified. He's even pissing himself, and the squad laughs at him.

LOGAN

Hahahaha, what a pussy!

BISHOP

Hey Logan, bet you five bucks this guy's got no prostate!

LOGAN

You're on.

Bishop shoots Abaddon in the crotch. He screams.

BISHOP

Pay up!

Logan laughs a bit, then grumbles and reaches into his pocket to give Bishop some money. Doc facepalms.

DOC CEDRICK

Humans...

As Abaddon holds his bloody crotch, whimpering, Doc holds a finger to his forehead and uses his powers to heal Abaddon. The pain subsides, but his pants are still bloody and he's still on the ground surrounded by corpses and still terrified. His goons are in no state to fight back.

MAX
(closing in on Abaddon with a drawn gun)
Alright Mr. Murdo, command wants you alive, but if you fuck around with us one more time, we'll make sure you lose your balls for real.

Logan looks confused, then turns to Bishop.

LOGAN
Hey give me back my money!

BISHOP
Fuck you! I didn't ask for interference!

MAX
Shut up! And you...
(turns to Abaddon)
Tell us what we want to know, now!

Abaddon points a shaking finger to the back of the warehouse.

ABADDON
It's all there, the real goods are back there.

MAX
That's not what we came for, you fucking fake! We want your contacts! Either spill the names or we spill your brains all over the place.

ABADDON

Alright, alright! I'll talk! Just don't kill me! Please!

MAX

(deactivating his gun)

Alright.

JILL

What a wuss. Wouldn't even be worth killing.

LOGAN

Aw, dammit, and I really wanted to eat this guy?

JILL

Why would you? Even I wouldn't touch that yellow bastard.

DOC CEDRICK

Don't we have a job to do?

MAX

Right. Grab him and the other survivors and get them to the transport.

As the squad takes Abaddon and the three goons, one of them tries to talk.

ABADDON GOON #1

Don't we have the right to an attorney?

BISHOP

No. Shut up. But I'll take your money.

Bishop reaches into the goon's pockets and takes some cash.

BISHOP

Abaddon's not paying you enough.

INT. POLICE HQ - INTERROGATION ROOM ANTECHAMBER - NIGHT

The interrogation room is nothing more than a table and some chairs. Abaddon is shackled in the chair talking to an Officer. The squad members are on the other side of a two-way mirror looking at him.

JILL

Look, he's still shaking.

BISHOP

Ugh, how does a guy like that become an arms dealer? He should be selling vacuum cleaners not guns.

DOC CEDRICK

He may have sloppy business plans, but he has quite a list of clientele.

Hartford bursts into the antechamber.

HARTFORD

You!

INT. POLICE HQ - INTERROGATION ROOM - NIGHT

Abaddon faces the interrogating Officer, DETECTIVE WHITE.

ABADDON

Alright, I admit this much. The weapons I was sell-ing to them were all defective. The real gear was in the back, beneath the floorboards. Start in the north

corner, and look for the marked board. It's all there.
The real deadly stuff.

DETECTIVE WHITE

We know all about that. What we want are the names
of your clients and their partners. Who did you sell
to?

ABADDON

Well, everyone really. Whoever had enough credits.
Local gangs, Mafia, even this one guy who said he just
wanted to protect his family.

DETECTIVE WHITE

Any real syndicates?

ABADDON

Uh... no.

DETECTIVE WHITE

Stop lying, ya scumbag.

ABADDON

I'm telling you, I don't know any syndicates!

Detective White fingers a button on a small remote, and the chains holding
Abaddon in the chair are electrified. He gets shocked, and screams in pain.

ABADDON

Okay, okay, I sold to Phalanx!

DETECTIVE WHITE

Who else?

ABADDON

Uh, the other guys, the scaleheads!

DETECTIVE WHITE

What's their organization named?

ABADDON

I don't know, I never met the guys! But I know who they're working with!

DETECTIVE WHITE

Who?

ABADDON

This guy, he's a drug maker. A chemist. Mixes up smack and sells it all over.

INT. POLICE HQ - INTERROGATION ROOM ANTECHAMBER - NIGHT

Hartford is furious, even more so than usual.

HARTFORD

Can't you misfit sons of bitches do anything right? You fucking freak bastards! I give you one simple assignment and you screw it all up! You shot an un-armed suspect and wagered on it!

LOGAN

Wait, how did you know that?

HARTFORD

This, asshole!

Hartford holds a comm device that is linked with the implants in each of the squad members' necks. The device is playing back key parts of the raid.

> LOGAN (V.O.)
> Hahahaha, what a pussy!

> BISHOP (V.O.)
> Hey Logan, bet you five bucks this guy's got no prostate!

> LOGAN (V.O.)
> You're on.

Sound of a gunshot and screaming.

> BISHOP (V.O.)
> Pay up!

Hartford turns off the comm. Logan is turning red.

> HARTFORD
> You sick bastards mutilated a suspect and wagered on it!

> DOC CEDRICK
> Ah, not entirely sir. I did heal him of his injury.

> HARTFORD
> I don't fucking care if you healed him of herpes! I said
> I wanted him alive! Not dead, and not injured!

> MAX
> Last time I saw, that's what we gave you. He's not dead, and
> he's not injured. He's still a coward, but we didn't do that.

LOGAN

What are you so pissed about? We got you your suspect, we got him alive, right? What else can you do against those psychopaths than sending other psychopaths after 'em? Makes perfect sense to the state's ideology, doesn't it?

HARTFORD

Don't patronize me, you fucking animal! You're all lucky I don't throw you in for execution right now!

MAX

Hey Chief, get some new material. You're getting old!

HARTFORD

Grrrr... <u>get out!</u>

INT. POLICE HQ - INTERROGATION ROOM - NIGHT
Abaddon looks around. He heard the echo of Hartford screaming.

ABADDON

What was that?

Detective White looks around too.

DETECTIVE WHITE

That's nothing. So tell me again about the Akaritan group.

INT. GPE - HESSMAN'S OFFICE - DAY
Hessman is at his office, reviewing some reports, browsing over research papers with the Asian market. Pike enters to deliver some files.

DR. PIKE

You said you needed these files?

HESSMAN

Yes Herbert, thank you very much.

Pike places a file disc on Hessman's desk.

DR. PIKE

Sir, if I may, why do need all the data on the mutants?

HESSMAN

Herbert, Chimara is close to being shut down by the board. We're too close now to be stopped by a bunch of relics who don't understand the future.

DR. PIKE

I don't understand. All the mutants in the country have been accounted for. After the mass executions, there haven't been many mutants left to cause trouble.

HESSMAN

That's beside the point, Herbert. Those mutants are the next step of the project. We need all the data we can get on them, every single one of them.

Pike is definitely suspicious about Hessman's plans.

HESSMAN

By the way, how is the progress on the cure developing?

DR. PIKE
(snaps back to attention)
Er, well, it's been difficult. The virus is actually quite resilient.

HESSMAN
What about bringing in live subjects?

DR. PIKE
We've done that already. They all died before we could start a test.

HESSMAN
Damn it, we need that cure, Dr. Pike, and we need it now!

DR. PIKE
I'm trying everything, Robert.

HESSMAN
Well, try harder! I didn't put you on this project to make us all look like fools!

DR. PIKE
Yes sir. I understand.

HESSMAN
Please leave. I need to start looking over the mutant files.

DR. PIKE
(nods)
Sir.

INT. GPE - PIKE'S LAB - MOMENTS LATER

Dr. Pike retreats to his lab. Rows of chemicals line the walls, as well as containment cells with plague-ridden bodies held in stasis. Dr. Pike collapses at his desk with a tired and worried look. He goes back to work on the cure, mixing some chemicals but they are all turning up negative changing color from red to black. He's getting more and more frustrated, then eventually tears himself away from the chemicals and goes to his computer. Dr. Pike brings up all of the files that he just gave Hessman out of curiosity.

> DR. PIKE
>
> Hmmm, all the mutant files. What does he want all this for?

He scrolls through files on the mutants, including physical signs, locations, accounts of recent attacks, but one file, one that he hasn't seen before, piques his interest. It's simply called "File 820" and when he tries to access it, he is met with "ACCESS DENIED" signs.

> DR. PIKE
>
> What? It's encrypted? I should have access to this, I'm a board member! What the hell?

He tries again and again to access File 820, but all his passwords don't work. He takes a deep breath and calls Doc Cedrick on the comm device.

> DR. PIKE
>
> Cornelius? It's Herbert. Listen, I've been working with Hessman at GPE on the viral spill, but for some reason he's been stocking up data on the mutants. I don't know why he wants it, but I think he's keeping something from me. I wish I could read his mind, but he's a hybrid, you know. Anyway, call me back as soon as you get this message. It's urgent.

INT. POLICE HQ - R&D LAB - DAY
Doc just got Dr. Pike's message, and puts down his comm device. He draws a
deep breath.

INT. POLICE HQ - BREAK ROOM - DAY
Max is eating a cold sandwich, Jill is lounging on a sofa smoking a cigarette,
and Bishop and Logan are arm-wrestling on a table a distance away from Max.
Bishop is winning.

> BISHOP
>
> Give it up, ya mutt!

> LOGAN
>
> I don't think so...!

Logan strains hard and pushes Bishop's arm down. With one last strain he wins
the game.

> LOGAN
>
> Yeah! Don't fuck with the wolf!
> (wolf howl)
>
> Arooooo!

> BISHOP
>
> (laughs)
>
> Cheers mother fucka.

Logan pours a shot of vodka from a bottle on the table and he and Bishop
toast then he downs it straight up. Bishop also takes a shot. Jill gets up and
takes the whole bottle and chugs it down like water. Logan and Bishop are
quite surprised.

LOGAN

Damn!

JILL

What? It's not blood baby. I can drink this like it's water.

Doc enters the room.

DOC CEDRICK

Jill, Logan, I need to talk to you for a few moments. Alone.

MAX

I got you.

BISHOP

Alright, I need to do something anyway. Be back in 10.

Max and Bishop step out of the room for a moment, leaving doc alone with Jill and Logan.

JILL

What do you need Doc?

DOC CEDRICK

I don't want the others to know. At least not yet.

LOGAN

How come you need to talk to just us?

DOC CEDRICK

I have just received news from my former colleague
Dr. Pike, that GPE is collecting mass databases on the
all mutants in the city.

LOGAN

What for? They're not planning another round of
mass executions, are they? I heard about those a while
ago.

DOC CEDRICK

Let's not jump to conclusions. It could be a security
measure against another series of mutations.

LOGAN

No kidding? My life's been hard enough looking like
this.
          (gestures to his face)
Now GPE wants to profile us all?

JILL

That's racist! Or is it like, uh, species-ist?

Logan laughs a bit. Doc isn't amused.

DOC CEDRICK

Listen, the reason I was put on an execution squad is
that when GPE took ownership of my people's tools
and technology, I was not about to let them be turned
into weapons, especially not to be used against us.
There were other Akaritans with me who tried to stop
them, but we were branded as terrorists and hunted

down. Like you and the others, my sentence was rehabilitation or death.

JILL

Gotta love how that corporation calls anyone who dis-
agrees with them terrorists.

DOC CEDRICK

I could not agree with you more. However, the fact
of the matter is that I believe they may be trying the
same thing again, only this time with the mutants. I
don't know exactly what that is, but my contact at GPE
is looking into a certain Project Chimera, which may
explain their interest in mutants.

LOGAN

Maybe we should tell Cain and Prescott? If anything
happens to us...

DOC CEDRICK

Not now, please. I have my reasons.

JILL

When then?

DOC CEDRICK

I need to get all the facts first from Dr. Pike. Until
then, if I ever find anything that would mean trouble
for you or the rest of the team, I give you my sacred
word of honor that I will alert you.

JILL

You mean the Akaritan have some decency in them?

DOC CEDRICK

Yes. The pure ones at least. Many of my people have been, unfortunately, corrupted by the economical and social structures of Earth. There are still others who spend their entire lives on the betterment of all species, filled with single-minded devotion to others. What you humans, I believe call <u>love</u>.

LOGAN

Good to know someone still cares.

DOC CEDRICK

I do my best.

Just then, Bishop and Max come back into the room

MAX

Had a nice chat?

LOGAN

Yeah.

MAX

Just got word from Hartford, we got a meeting. Squad room. Like now.

JLL

Just for us?

BISHOP

Everyone, the whole force. It's got to be something big.

The group heads to the squad room down the hallway with other regular police officers and separate Executioner Squad teams.

INT. MAIN SQUAD MEETING ROOM - NIGHT
All the cops in the room including the convict squad teams stand before Hartford like the judge he is. He directs their attention to the screen on the wall with a video hologram projector showing maps of the city with syndicate locations highlighted in different colors.

> HARTFORD
>
> All right people, listen up! We have reports coming in from uptown about new syndicates moving in. But what is more important is that we have some fresh intel on Phalanx, no thanks to the freak squad in the second back row.

Max and the others of their quintet smirk. All except Doc Cedrick of course.

> HARTFORD
>
> Detective White has gotten our old friend Mr. Murdo, Abaddon, to talk and has revealed to us that the syndicates are the ones who are supplying the Phalanx with weapons. Pretty soon there could be a full-blown war in the city. Orders have come down from the top: all known Phalanx members, either in custody or at large, are to be shot on sight. No mercy, no sympathy. And don't let any of them try to bargain with you, or else you'll be no better off than they are. I want Phalanx completely taken down, all of it.

> OFFICER
>
> What about Murdo?

HARTFORD

We could've gotten more out of him, but it turns out that spineless asshole has got a relative who just so happens to be a diplomat. We had no choice but to release him.

The whole squad room is shocked.

MAX

What the hell? This is bullshit!

HARTFORD

For once Prescott I actually agree with you. But it's all out of our hands. For now all of you get going and keep the airwaves open. Go kill me some Phalanx members. Dismissed!

The entire squad room departs and goes to hunt. Except Max and his team.

HARTFORD

Prescott, you and your team stay put. I'm not done with you yet.

MAX

Great, what did we do now?

HARTFORD

For once, a good job. I'm impressed. You brought Murdo in, and we got a lot of good information. The five of you take the night off. Get some rest. You earned it.

LOGAN

You're kidding, right?

HARTFORD

No I'm not. I want the five of you to go home and take
a break. That's an order.

Max and his crew trade confused looks at each other, then shrug and
walk out the door, leaving Hartford standing there, looking sour in their
direction.

EXT. HELL'S KITCHEN - MAX'S APARTMENT - NIGHT
Max shuffles to the front door of his apartment complex, a dumpy brick building in the middle of a really bad neighborhood. He fumbles with the electronic
card-key reader.

INT. HELL'S KITCHEN - MAX'S APARTMENT - MOMENTS LATER
Max walks into his apartment, still confused about what Hartford said and still
mad that Abaddon got away. His room is filled with trash, cigarette butts and
alcohol bottles. There are government-installed cameras in every corner of the
room. He picks a bottle up off the floor, grabs a dirty shot glass among the trash
and pours himself a drink and downs it. He then collapses on a filthy sofa and
pours yet another drink, gulping it quickly.

MAX

(imitating Hartford)

"Go kill me some Phalanx members... but not you
guys. You did a good job for once, go home." The hell
is he playing at?

INT. DOWNTOWN - BISHOP'S APARTMENT - NIGHT
Bishop walks in to a slightly more well-kept apartment. There are pictures of his
family, a wife and two sons, including past military medals adorning the walls, as
well as a few cameras in the corners. A beagle trots up to him, and Bishop picks
him up and starts patting him.

                              BISHOP
        Hey boy!

Bishop walks over to an old beat-up holograph set and turns it on. A news segment is just ending.

                          REPORTER #1
        ...since the first arrival of the Akaritan race on Earth in
        2044. Some have claimed that the assimilation of the
        Akaritans into human society was a conspiracy to stage
        what was deemed a silent revolution to usurp control
        in the worldwide political stage. These groups have
        since merged into the human-only syndicate known as
        Phalanx, whose agenda is characterized by acts of vio-
        lence against Akaritans, especially those in any kind of
        authority position over humans.

                       PHALANX HUMAN #1
        Goddamn scaleheads want to take our planet right out
        from underneath us! They invaded Congress, they in-
        vaded the UN, now they're invading our cities and our
        homes! They're robbing us all of our ability to call our
        own shots! And then they tried turning us into abomi-
        nations with their mutation projects! They're all out to
        enslave us! We must rise up and defend the planet that
        God made us the masters of! Humans forever! Hail
        Phalanx!

Bishop scoffs at the news report, cradling his dog.

                              BISHOP
        Ugh, I wish I could kill that guy.

INT. UPTOWN - DOC'S PENTHOUSE - NIGHT

Doc lives in a spacious, well-kept penthouse. There are fully stocked bookshelves and postmodern-design furniture -- and surveillance cameras. He reclines on a bright green sofa and turns on his comm device.

> ### DOC CEDRICK
>
> Herbert? It's Cornelius again. I've already informed the two mutant members of my squad about our suspicions with GPE. The sooner we can unveil some facts about their plans, the more I hope to be able to relax. Call me as soon as you can.

Doc hangs up and turns on a radio on a small glass table. The sounds of Antonio Vivaldi's "Four Seasons" (Allegro-Spring) fills the room, and doc heaves a sigh.

INT. CHINATOWN - LOGAN'S ROOM - NIGHT

Logan lives in a small room in a Buddhist monastery. While some monks are chanting down the hall, Logan retreats to his room, which is filled with weight sets and exercise equipment. Mounted on the walls are some fighting championship belts and medals, and some framed photos of Logan with Mob bosses and an his best friend, a fellow fighter and rival. In a corner is a Buddhist shrine. There are also surveillance cameras. Logan takes a photo of his friend off the wall and looks at it with regret.

> ### LOGAN
>
> Joey, I'm sorry man. What went down that night in the ring I wish never happened. I shouldn't have fought you. Now you're dead and I am here. You should be alive, not me. I deserve to die for all the things I've done.
> (beat)
> You were a great guy and look what I've become... a freaking monster.

He turns to the Buddha statue and rings a bell next to it, centering himself in prayer.

INT. MIDTOWN - THE NAPALM ROCK CLUB - NIGHT
The Napalm Rock Club is filled with loud music and rambunctious crowds. A large mosh pit is forming in front of the stage as a band of human and mutant punks are shredding on guitars and pounding on drums.

INT. JILL'S LOFT - MOMENTS LATER
Jill's loft above the club is filled with Goth accessories. The music from the club can be heard booming through the walls. Jill is wearing a skimpy bikini made of black leather. She opens a small mini-fridge and grabs a blood packet, ripping it open and drinking deeply. There is a man (human) sitting in a chair against the opposite wall who looks very horny. Jill turns to him with a devilish look.

                         JILL
          You know what I'm thirsty for, babe?

                        DONOR
          Oh yeah.

                         JILL
              (walking up to him, licking her lips)
          You gonna give me some?

                        DONOR
          Yeah, you can have it all, honey!

Jill sits in the donor's lap and rubs him sensually. The man is loving it. She grabs his right arm and licks the bare skin, then sinks her fangs into his forearm. The man screams as blood seeps out of the wound that Jill begins to suckle at hungrily. The donor is a masochist; the pain is so sweet to him. His free hand is caressing her body as she continues to suck at the wound. When Jill has had her fill, she exhales with pleasure and starts taking off her top. The donor is undressing as well, his arm still bloody. Surveillance cameras are capturing all of the action. Jill and the donor get naked and have passionate sex. They are both very much into each other. Her sweet embrace is deep and romantic as if flowers are blooming made of light and fire.

> DONOR
> (breathing deep)
> Damn girl... Hell, you're amazing.

> JILL
> (breathing as she is doing him)
> Shut up and make love to me.

They continue to make love for a while then stop.

INT. JILL'S LOFT - LATER
An hour has passed and it is late at night around 11PM. The two lovers rest after having hot times. The donor really likes her.

> DONOR
> Hey, what's your name?

> JILL
> (annoyed)
> Why the hell do you care?

> DONOR
> Nothing, it's just... you were great.

                              JILL
                    (coldly and sarcastic)
          Thanks, I guess. It's just business. You got what you
          wanted and I got what I needed.

                              DONOR
          Hey I just wanted to get to know you.

                              JILL
          Jill.
                              (beat)
          You?

                              JACK
          Jack.

                              JILL
          That's funny.

Jack looks on the side of Jill's nightstand and sees a picture of Jill with a little
girl.

                              JACK
          That your daughter?

                              JILL
          Yeah.

A beat.

> JILL
> (upset)

She's dead. Gang scaleheads, killed her. The cops didn't do anything about it.

> JACK

I'm sorry.

> JILL
> (coldly)

Get out.

> JACK
> (pissed)

Crazy bitch.

Jill gets pissed, jumps on Jack and morphs into her more vampiric nature. A she-devil mad as hell. Showing her demonic fangs and face. Her eyes glowing with flames.

> JILL
> (screams)

Get out or I'll kill you!!!

Jack falls off the bed in fear and quickly heads to the door with his clothes in his hands, while still naked. Exit stage left.

> JACK

Freak!

He leaves slamming the door behind him.

Jill gets up and grabs her small vase and flings it at the door smashing it, yelling out.

JILL
(screams)

Fuck you!!!

EXT. HELL'S KITCHEN - MAX'S APARTMENT - NIGHT

Max is still up, insomnia, is the side effect of his ill depressed life. Frustration feeds his thoughts as he sits on his couch having a electronic cigarette -- being stuck in the squad program, having to risk death on a daily basis with his reluctant job, treated like shit by Hartford and having nothing to look forward to in life if he survives his tour of duty other than a release in his mid-fifties and diminishing pension to live off of. Stated, a wasted meaningless existence. Suddenly, all of a sudden, something is thrown through the glass window shattering it. It's a grenade!

MAX

Shit!!!

Max dives out of the room out into the hall as the grenade explodes.

KABOOM!

Shards of glass and a splintered wooden door fragments are in the hall.

INT. HALLWAY - NIGHT

Max takes off down the hall running, as his neighbors open their doors. Only to scream at the sight of two masked hit men in trench coats walking into view, carrying machine guns. They open fire, killing the neighbors with no regard. They drop like flies, unintentionally shielding Max.

Max dives out of the hall window landing into the fire escape, still armed as with his gun.

EXT. FIRE ESCAPE - NIGHT
He ducks under the old brick window seal for some protection and fires back, hitting one of the hit men in the head -- who had run in his direction thinking their target fell to his death.

INT. HALLWAY - NIGHT
The other hit man is distracted as his gun jams -- Max goes in for the kill, disarming the other hit man and shooting him in the chest multiple times. Blood spurts in bursts over the walls spraying them red. Max looks down to see a car that was below his window speed off.

EXT. FIRE ESCAPE - NIGHT
Max runs down the fire escape to the street level.

EXT. STREET - NIGHT
On the street, Max steals a parked car. He smashes its window open and hotwires it with a shaved key in his pocket. He uses it if he has to "commandeer" a vehicle as a cop. He takes off.

INT. MAX'S STOLEN CAR - NIGHT
Max whips out his comm device and calls Jill. He keeps his composure. Just like the soldier that he is. Calm and collected. He speeds through the streets among other cars in the borough. The traffic is light. But to his surprise Jill calls him first.

JILL (V.O.)
Max it's me. Some bastards broke into my place and tried to kill me.

MAX
You too!

JILL (V.O.)

What are you talking about?

MAX

Someone threw a grenade in my place nearly blowing me up. Then two shooters came in to finish me off.

JILL (V.O.)

Are you alright?

MAX

I killed both of them and managed to get away. Where are you right now?

JILL (V.O.)

At Logan's. I hitched a train to Chinatown. He's with me right now. Doc and Bishop, the same thing happened to them also. They managed to get out of there alive. We're all pretty lucky, including yourself.

MAX

Someone set us up.

JILL (V.O.)

Who? Almost every creep in this town has it in for us. Who do you think it is.

MAX

Let me think for a second. Anyway where are Doc and Bishop?

JILL (V.O.)

On the other side of town, they are on their way here.

MAX

Did anything go down at Logan's?

INT. CHINATOWN - LOGAN'S ROOM - NIGHT
Jill is on the phone talking.

INTERCUT TELEPHONE CONVERSATION.

JILL

No. This is Triad territory, it's under protection.

MAX

What about the guys who attacked you?

JILL

I killed them. Ripped them apart. Then I split.

MAX

It has to be Hartford. Why else would that fat ass
send us home for the night? It felt too convenient,
weird.

JILL

How are we going to prove it? Even if it's true?
Everyone will take his side over ours.

MAX

I don't know.

EXT. CHINATOWN - NIGHT
Max parks his car on the street and heads to over to the Buddhist monastery. He
knocks on the large entrance door and a peephole slides open revealing to us two
eyes looking at him behind the main door.

                    MONK (V.O.)
Who you? This place is off limits to the public.

                        MAX
I'm here to see Logan. Police business. He's one of my
teammates.

Max flashes his badge to the monk.

                    MONK (V.O.)
Oh you, Prescott? He'd said you come.

The door opens to reveal an old Buddhist monk in robe and garb holding a lit
oil lantern to greet Prescott.

                        MONK
Please, come in.

INT. CHINATOWN MONASTERY - MAIN SHRINE ROOM - NIGHT
Max enters the monastery with the monk closing the door behind them. The
two enter into a grand candle-lit shrine room with a giant brass Buddha in the
center of the room with an altar. Burning incense is on the altar and a bowl of
fruit as an offering. The walls are adorned by marble circular pillars with jade
dragon statues wrapped around them. Max looks in awe.

                        MAX
Nice place.

                        MONK
This way if you please. Mr. Prescott.

INT. MONASTERY HALLWAY - NIGHT
The monk leads Max down the lantern lit hallway to Logan's room and lets Max in. Then shuts the door and leaves.

INT. CHINATOWN - LOGAN'S ROOM - NIGHT
Inside the room Bishop and Doc are there along with Logan and Jill present. Eager to come up with a solution and find out who tried to kill them. Logan kneels at his shrine.

MAX

Is everyone alright?

LOGAN
(not looking up)

I'm okay.

JILL

Those fuckers... they broke into my room!

DOC CEDRICK

Calm down, Jill.

JILL

Don't tell me to be calm! I'm gonna kill those bastards who did it!

DOC CEDRICK

I thought you already did.

Jill exhales and flops down on the floor, restless.

MAX

Doc? You alright?

BISHOP

Is he alright? I got shot in my own place, and you're asking is he alright?

MAX

Okay, okay, Bishop, how about you?

BISHOP
(rubbing his shoulder)
Copped one back at my place. Some asshole with a rifle busted in to my room and tore up the place. But I'll be alright.

DOC CEDRICK

If I may?

Doc walks over to Bishop and heals him. Bishop sighs, feeling the pain leaving him. Jill is pacing around the room, frustrated.

JILL

Who could've done this? Who could've known where we all live?

MAX

I told you already, it had to have been Hartford.

BISHOP

Hartford?!

MAX

Yeah. Why else would he send us all home instead of going after Phalanx? It had to have been him!

DOC CEDRICK

That makes no sense. We are all still indentured to the state, and considering our combat record, they've no legitimate reason to do away with some of their finest.

JILL

He's right, it could've been someone we took down a while ago, maybe an old splinter faction trying to get back at us after we took down their leaders or something. God, I want to rip their hearts out!

BISHOP

Wouldn't surprise me. Could've been that little dumb-shit Abaddon.

MAX
(laughs sarcastically)
No. It's Hartford, I know it.

DOC CEDRICK

On what evidence, Max?

MAX
(at a loss)
I... I don't know, it's just, it feels like him.

BISHOP

How?

MAX

Well, when was the last time he told us we did a good job? Or sending us home instead of working with the rest of the force when they've got their hands full?

JILL

You're full of shit, Max! Those guys that jumped me in my room, they were not cops!

MAX

(getting frustrated)
Well, maybe he's hired some hitmen!

DOC CEDRICK

If Hartford tried to kill us, he would be answering to the board! He wouldn't stake his reputation to rid himself of us!

MAX

(shouting)
I'm telling you, <u>it's him!</u>

Logan gets up from his shrine angrily.

LOGAN

Will you fuckers keep it down?! I'm trying to get some enlightenment here!

Max exhales as Logan turns back to his meditation. Max tries to compose himself.

MAX

Look, don't ask me how I know this, I just do, okay?
Call it instinct. It's all just really suspicious, alright?

Max looks over at Logan, noticing the implant mark on the back of his neck.

MAX

And if those things in our necks still work, Hartford
knows we're still alive.

JILL

I told you, the Triads have got this place protected.
There's no way they can get us here.

BISHOP

I say we shack up here for the night, and save it for the
morning to kick Hartford's fat ass.

LOGAN
(rising)

My place, my rules.

BISHOP

What, you're kicking us out?

LOGAN

No. I think Max is on to something. It's obvious
Hartford's not really our best friend, and we could've
had better things to do than go home. I say we wait
until morning. Hartford goes back in his office and

meets with some board members tomorrow. If it is him behind it, he wouldn't try to kill us again with everyone watching.

DOC CEDRICK

Brilliant notion.

MAX

Alright. So, tomorrow? When he's meeting with the board members?

Logan nods.

INT. HARTFORD'S OFFICE - MORNING
Hartford walks in with two board members, Goldstein and Lylesberg. Hartford collapses at his desk.

HARTFORD

Alright, what did they do this time?

MR. GOLDSTEIN

It's not about 0257 at all, Hartford. It's about you.

HARTFORD

What about me?

MR. LYLESBERG

We've been monitoring your bank account recently, Chief Hartford, and we've found some inaccuracies.

HARTFORD

What are you doing snooping around my bank account?

MR. GOLDSTEIN
You know full well that all public employees are moni-
tored. And would you care to explain those deposits
made by GPE to your account?

HARTFORD
I don't know what you're talking about.

MR. LYLESBERG
Chief Hartford, if we find out that you have been ac-
cepting bribes --

HARTFORD
(cuts in)
You've got nothing to charge me with. You have no
evidence!

MR. GOLDSTEIN
Yes we do!

Goldstein pulls up a portable computer, and brings up Hartford's bank state-
ment. He scrolls through some text on the screen, but to his dismay there's nothing with GPE's name on it. He runs a search "Recent Deposits," and they are all
from the City of New York. Nothing from GPE.

HARTFORD
Like I said, you can't charge me with taking bribes.

Goldstein looks lost and frustrated. Whatever evidence there was is gone. Max
barges into the room.

MAX
How about attempted murder?

The board members are stunned. Hartford is furious.

HARTFORD

What the hell are you talking about?

Max is pissed off too. He draws a gun and aims it at Hartford's head. Instantly the board members and two cops nearby draw their weapons. It's a standoff.

MAX

You sent assassins after me and the rest of my team!

HARTFORD

I... don't know what you're talking about.

Max jams the muzzle of the gun into Hartford's forehead. The others look ready to shoot.

MAX

You sent us all home last night, and only you know
where we all live. Who else could've done this?

HARTFORD
(through clenched teeth)
Get that gun out of my face, you piece of shit!

Max looks around at all the guns pointed at him. Instantly Hartford grabs Max's wrist and disarms him. The gun clatters to the floor. While Max is in a scramble to grab it, Hartford takes something out of his pocket, a small console with some buttons and dials on it. He pushes a button, and instantly Max is incapacitated, as if he's being shocked with 10,000 volts.

Max screams in pain!

Hartford takes his thumb off a button on the device. Max is sprawled on the floor in agony.

HARTFORD

Remember that implant in your neck?

Max growls in pain.

HARTFORD
(shows device)

This button...

(points to a button)

...will kill you. And this one...

(points to another button)

...will make you wish I did.

Hartford hovers over Max, looking like a monolith.

HARTFORD

So you see, I don't even need to send hitmen if I wanted to kill you. I could've killed you and the rest of your
freakshow anytime I wanted. You forget that I hold all
the cards.

Hartford turns to the two board members, still in the room.

HARTFORD

And speaking of which, you know you can't charge me
with bribery. But you can sure as hell charge them!

MR. GOLDSTEIN

What do you mean?

HARTFORD

Unlike you bureaucratic twerps, I actually do have evidence against this squad.

Hartford turns to his desk and taps on a computer terminal. Instantly, the room is filled with the sound of a recording from a previous mission.

ABADDON GOON #1 (V.O.)
Don't we have the right to an attorney?

BISHOP (V.O.)
No. Shut up. But I'll take your money.

Sound of Bishop reaching into the goon's pockets.

BISHOP (V.O.)
Abaddon's not paying you enough.

The board members, and Max, are both stunned. Hartford grins evilly.

HARTFORD
Another little feature to remind you who's boss. I can record every word you say. Anytime, anyplace. And that includes this!

Hartford skips ahead in the recording, and lets it play at:

JILL (V.O.)
Who could've done this? Who could've known where we all live?

MAX (V.O.)
I told you already, it had to have been Hartford.

BISHOP (V.O.)
Hartford?!

MAX (V.O.)

Yeah. Why else would he send us all home instead of
going after Phalanx? It had to have been him!

Hartford looks smug.

HARTFORD

Yeah, I knew you were going to accuse me. Between that
and taking a bribe from Abaddon's lackey, I'd say that this
team has reached the end of its rope. What do you say?

The board members are puzzled, but Lylesberg steps forward.

MR. LYLESBERG

Max Prescott, leader of Executioner Squad 0257, in light
of this new evidence of bribery and insubordination...

Max looks ready for a death sentence, and Hartford is loving the scene unfold-
ing. He's happy that he's finally getting to stick it to the squad.

MR. LYLESBERG

...we will place you and the rest of your squad on indefi-
nite suspension and house arrest.

Hartford explodes.

HARTFORD

What?!

MR. GOLDSTEIN

Considering your service record, and recent victory in
bringing the arms dealer Abaddon to justice, I agree

with Mr. Lylesberg's decision. The rest of the board will concur.

HARTFORD
Are you out of your fucking mind?! He tried to kill me!

MR. GOLDSTEIN
Hartford, we know you're just as guilty as him, and mark my words we will find out what's going on.

Hartford shrinks down at these words, sulking back to his desk.

MR. GOLDSTEIN
And unless you want Internal Affairs breaking down your door, you would do well to abide by our decision.

Goldstein turns to Max, who's regained his footing. Hartford is busy at his computer.

MR. GOLDSTEIN
And you and the rest of the team will be put on suspension. You will turn in all weapons and you are not to leave your residences under any circumstances.

MAX
A vacation?

MR. LYLESBERG
You will stay in your home, and don't even consider trying to get out.

MAX

And never mind the fact that my place was just bombed
to hell, right?

MR. GOLDSTEIN

In that case, you will reside with Mr. Kennedy in
Chinatown.

MAX

No way, I hate that place. It smells.

MR. LYLESBERG

Too bad.

Hartford interrupts.

HARTFORD

Wait! I think there might be one last job for this team.

The phone on Hartford's desk rings.

HARTFORD
(annoyed)

Actually everyone get out. I need to take this call.

Max and the board members and other cops leave. Hartford is alone. He picks
up the phone.

HARTFORD

Hartford here.

HESSMAN (V.O.)
Chief Hartford, it's Robert Hessman calling.

Hartford is suddenly scared.

HARTFORD
Hessman... I think the board's getting suspicious of
me. From now on I want you to send someone to my
private residence with cash.

HESSMAN (V.O.)
Duly noted. As long as you keep your end of the
bargain.

HARTFORD
Don't I always?

HESSMAN (V.O.)
You have so far, but there is something we need from you.

HARTFORD
Alright, who do you want this time?

HESSMAN (V.O.)
We found Philip Walton, the one you call code-name
Bacchus.

HARTFORD
The drug baron? What do you want with him?

HESSMAN (V.O.)
I want you to simply enforce the law, of course. Take
him down.

HARTFORD

Is that all?

HESSMAN (V.O.)

Bacchus has stolen something that is GPE property. I want it back, or it could endanger all of our research. Send your best team to kill him and his affiliates.

HARTFORD

I know just the team. They're a real bunch of psychopaths.

HESSMAN (V.O.)

You don't mean <u>those</u> psychopaths, do you?

HARTFORD

Just let me handle it. I'll take care of this.

HESSMAN (V.O.)

See that you do. I'll know if anything happens.

INT. MAIN SQUAD MEETING ROOM - MOMENTS LATER

In the meeting room, the Squad gathers to hear about their latest assignment. The screen on the far end of the room is aglow with the face of a half-breed man.

HARTFORD

Philip Walton, code-name Bacchus. He's a drug baron operating out of the midtown boroughs. We have it on good authority that the plague may have started from one of his drugs.

MAX

Another kill operation?

HARTFORD

Not entirely. Bacchus is keeping something in his base of operations, experimental chemicals. I can't overstate how important it is for you to recover those chemicals.

DOC CEDRICK

Do you mean a cure for the plague?

HARTFORD

With any luck, yes. This could be the turning point in stopping the disease. So don't you dare screw this one up!

JILL

Chief, why are you sending us after some stupid chemicals? Isn't that what HAZMAT was for?

HARTFORD

Shut up! If we miss this, then there'll be no chance at stopping the plague! Now get to work!

LOGAN

Dude, we're not even getting workman's comp for this shit.

Hartford growls and points at the door. The Squad leaves.

INT. GPE BOARDROOM - MORNING

There is another board meeting under way. Human and Akaritan investors are present at this meeting. Hessman is still conspicuously absent. The board members are arguing viciously about how to deal with Hessman. Snyder is sitting in a corner watching the show. Gene is trying to restore order.

GENE

Gentlemen, please! Can we focus?

BOARD MEMBER #1

We should lock him out! He's ruining the whole company!

BOARD MEMBER #2

We're losing millions of dollars every day gentleman! Millions! This is an outrage!

BOARD MEMBER #3

We should sue him! Now we got activists and religious zealots protesting at our gates and our stock is in the sewers! If this keeps up, we'll all be out of business!

Other shouts erupt through the room.

BOARDMEMBERS

Fire him! / Sue him! / Arrest that son of a bitch! / Half-breed bastard!

...And other more colorful lines that one wouldn't expect businessmen to say. Gene is still trying to calm them.

GENE

Gentlemen, calm down! I think I know how to deal with this!

The room does get somewhat calmer.

GENE

I've contacted several investors from overseas. They've agreed to pool their resources and buy back Hessman's stock in the company. He'll be out before you know it.

Snyder takes a stand.

SNYDER

Gentlemen, I must protest. Robert Hessman has made this company into the powerhouse that it is today! We've made billions thanks to his contributions, and so what if a little plague got out? Without his expertise we wouldn't be one of the most powerful corporations on the planet! You owe him another chance!

Everyone looks at him like he said something really stupid.

GENE

Mr. Snyder, we can no longer afford such embarrassments. As much as we care about our profit margins, Hessman has broken our every mandate about advancing both our species. He's turned humans and Akaritans into abominations! If he wants to play god, let it be on someone else's dime, not ours!

Hessman walks in, late as usual.

HESSMAN

Playing is for children, my friend.

The board is furious.

GENE

Robert, we have already brokered a deal and we're buying you out! You're finished with this company, effec-
tive immediately!

Hessman lights up a cigarette, smoking nonchalantly. He's not interested in what
he's being told.

GENE

Are you listening?! You are no longer vice chairman of
this company, and we are taking back all of our assets
right now! You're done with Project Chimara, you're
done with GPE -- you're fired!

HESSMAN
(after a pause)

So be it.

Hessman leaves the room, and Snyder, after flashing the board a sour look,
leaves with him. The board turns to each other.

BOARD MEMBER #1

Hmm, well that was easy.

BOARD MEMBER #2

Too easy.

INT. GPE - HESSMAN'S OFFICE - MOMENTS LATER

Hessman is packing his briefcase and transferring files on the GPE server
from his computer. He doesn't look the least bit worried, but Snyder certainly
does.

SNYDER

What? Aren't you going to fight back? Are you letting them do this to us, Robert?

HESSMAN

Don't worry. Every ending is a new beginning.

SNYDER

What? So we are leaving the company?

Hessman taps a few keys on the computer console.

HESSMAN

Do you believe in fate, Lawrence?

SNYDER

No I don't. Just some bullshit people make up to make themselves think something's happening for a reason.

HESSMAN

Things <u>do</u> happen for a reason, Lawrence. All the time.

SNYDER

Seriously?

HESSMAN

Since we're free of the board's control, how about dinner at your home tonight?

SNYDER

What's to celebrate? We've lost our project and our money!

HESSMAN

Trust me.

INT. LONG ISLAND - SNYDER'S HOME - EVENING

Snyder has a really fancy home, very posh, which annoys Hessman a bit. The furniture and decor are mostly Victorian, with lots of expensive antiques on display. Snyder and Hessman are in a study, sipping wine and smoking.

HESSMAN
(facing a large window)
Advancement... the board kept talking about that endlessly. But they never knew the meaning of it.

SNYDER

What do you mean, sir?

HESSMAN

Advancement is not something that can be bought or sold. Advancement is not a product. It is the work of fate. It is the survival of the fittest, and the world has seemed to forget that.

SNYDER
(yawning)
I hate it when you give sermons. I don't do philosophy, I do business. I'm here to make money.

HESSMAN
(annoyed)
And we will, Lawrence. Far more than peddling stolen Akaritan devices and slapping a patent on them.

SNYDER
(on the offensive)

Hey!

HESSMAN

Relax...

Hessman walks over to Snyder.

HESSMAN

Advancement is what I have dedicated my life towards. My family was built upon it. My father was a human, a powerful Senator. My mother was a high priestess to the Akaritan gods. They both worked for better worlds for both races on Earth.

SNYDER

And did they?

HESSMAN

No. They were murdered. My mother by human gangs, and my father by Akaritans.

SNYDER
(trying to sound sympathetic)

I'm sorry.

HESSMAN

Don't be. Their deaths gave me a purpose. And that purpose led to Project Chimara in the first place.

SNYDER

How the hell does making mutants have to do with that?

HESSMAN

Think about it. For all this time, the humans and
Akaritans have been bickering all over the world over
who really owns it. Even before their arrival, even humans themselves have fought each other over lands,
money, supremacy, anything. But I will change all of
that. I will change everything.

Snyder chokes on his drink.

HESSMAN

Imagine, a world of one people, one race. There won't
be any more discrimination or infighting. No preju-
dice or racism. There would be nothing left to fight
about. No more differences to divide anyone. Humans,
Akaritans, they will both be made to perfection! To
real advancement! And anyone who refuses it will die,
exactly as it should be!

Snyder can't believe what he just heard.

SNYDER

So you're going to rule the world with your master race?

HESSMAN

Who said anything about ruling them? They can finally be able to rule themselves and build a lasting
peace. After everyone is changed I will step down and
let the people rule, as they should. No longer will ty-
rants and world leaders, whose corruption has moved
the earth, destroy the balance of world's society. No...
the people shall rule it alone. Together, united with
one voice. One people.

SNYDER

And what are we doing when this happens? Will that include us too?

HESSMAN

Of course. Everyone wants equality. We'll they'll get it.

SNYDER

(getting up)

Robert, I don't want equality. I want control. I want it all.

HESSMAN

(sighing)

Still preoccupied with money, are we? Is that all you care about?

SNYDER

It's not that, it's just... well what else is there?

HESSMAN

Bear with me, and you'll have more money than ever, my friend.

SNYDER

What? You'll charge people for turning into mutants?

HESSMAN

No! Something better. Something that will start...

(checks his watch)

...in about two minutes.

SNYDER
(looks at his watch)
What happens then?

HESSMAN
Just turn on your holograph set, and see for yourself.

Snyder turns on the news. There's a report about a terrorist battle gone wrong.

REPORTER #1 (V.O.)
That's the scene here in New York, as a massive police offensive against the terrorist organization called Phalanx has ended in tragedy. Phalanx forces have claimed more ground against the police. It's a losing battle for the NYPD here.

Hessman chuckles.

HESSMAN
Ah, they told me they were good enough to take the whole city.

SNYDER
Is that what you wanted to show me?

HESSMAN
No. It should be coming up right about...
(checks his watch)
...now.

REPORTER #1 (V.O.)

Um, wait... we've received breaking news. Global Placement Enterprises, GPE, just suffered a massive loss. I'm being told their stock just crashed to zero, and the entire board of directors is in complete chaos.

The scene changes to outside GPE's headquarters, where the board members are fleeing the place while mobs of angry investors are rampaging through the area. Hordes of white-collar investors are shooting board members in the streets. Cars are being torched, and armed mobs are storming GPE.

On the screen is an interior of GPE's board room, which has turned into a full-on brawl with the board members and an armed mob. Some board members are wrestling with investors, and they crash into a window and plummet 150 stories down.

REPORTER #1 (V.O.)

It is complete anarchy here at GPE's headquarters. Almost makes the Phalanx attack look tame. I'm being told that a state of emergency is being declared, and there are now Executioner Squads called in to suppress the rioting.

Onscreen, a certain Akaritan board member is being shot full of holes by an angry mob.

SNYDER

Hey, is that Gene?

HESSMAN

Yes. He looks much better that way, doesn't he?

Snyder turns to Hessman with a worried look.

SNYDER

You said I'd be getting money out of this! If the company's broke...

HESSMAN

I told you to trust me. I left a small going-away present on the computer servers before I left the office. A virus that would load into all computer servers on the world wide web. Nothing can stop it. Only I have the code. It was timed to trigger exactly as I said. That's how all of their money vanished before their eyes.

SNYDER

And where is it?

HESSMAN

Offshore accounts in Europe and Asia. Multi-shell corporations in the thousands. Electronically set up and already filled with the combined fortunes of everyone at GPE, including the late Mr. Gene and our friends from the board. A little insurance I had set up a two years ago, just to make sure everything would go according to plan.

Snyder lights up.

SNYDER

Billions?

HESSMAN

Trillions.

Snyder hesitates, then laughs maniacally. On the holograph, the scene changes to other locations around the country, where mass rioting is under way at other GPE-owned locations. It's an official stock-market crash, and the whole country is in panic.

> REPORTER #1 (V.O.)
> GPE owns massive resource deposits and technology foundries all over the country, and now that the company has gone bankrupt, millions of people are displaced and out of work, losing their livelihood and investments, and they've taken to the streets.

Onscreen, flipping through different channels shows the same images of people rioting and looting storefronts, stealing weaponry and heavy military-grade arms (rockets, machine guns, etc.). Said weapons are being fired by civilians and Executioner Squads alike in open combat.

> REPORTER #1 (V.O.)
> As you can see, there is absolute chaos in the streets. People are armed and there are clashes with police and Executioner -- AAH!

Reporter #1 gets shot among the crowds. The camera jostles around.

> SNYDER
> Robert, you're a fucking genius!

> HESSMAN
> (smiling)
> I know. And this is only the beginning.

He pulls out a ringing comm device.

HESSMAN

Hang on a sec. Need to take this call.
(turns on the comm)
Hessman.

Hartford is on the other line.

HARTFORD (V.O.)

Hessman! What the hell just happened?!

Hessman has to hold his head away from the comm, Hartford is really shouting.

HESSMAN

Joseph, please calm down.

HARTFORD (V.O.)

Calm down?! You want me to calm down?! The whole damn city is going to hell, we've got no manpower left and you want me to calm down?!

HESSMAN

I've gone into business for myself. Your payments will still be delivered.

HARTFORD (V.O.)

That's not the point! Right now I could care less. GPE's gone bankrupt and now everyone's taken to the streets! It's not just here in New York, it's everywhere. We've got mass riots all over the damn country! What am I supposed to do?

HESSMAN

Leave it to me. All I need is some time to make the
arrangements.

Hessman hangs up. He just bankrupted one of the world's biggest corporations
and threw the country into a mass panic, and he celebrates by sipping some wine.
This is only the beginning...

EXT. MIDTOWN - BACCHUS'S LAIR - NIGHT

On the streets of New York, the Squad piles out of their tank and out into a
high-class neighborhood.

BISHOP

How do you find a drug baron in a place like this?
What is he, a stockbroker?

MAX

Who cares? Let's just find this guy and get it over with.

Max heads over to the target's address, followed by his team in ready formation.
He opens the door -- it's unlocked -- and they head inside. Down a long hall, there
is an elevator door flanked by two armed guards. They point their weapons at the
Squad, who do likewise. There is a standoff, and the guards withdraw suddenly.

BISHOP

(looking back at Max)

What the hell?

GUARD #1

(into comm device)

Team One, stand down. Our guests have arrived.

LOGAN
Guests? What's going on?

MAX
Might be a trap. Stay on your guard.

GUARD #2
We've been expecting someone from the police force here. He's downstairs waiting for you.

The Squad slowly walks past the guards and into the spacious elevator. It closes and heads down.

DOC CEDRICK
Something doesn't feel right.

JILL
(condescending)
Thank you Captain Obvious. So what now? Do we still shoot this guy or what?

MAX
We should probably focus on getting the chemicals first, if they're that important.

The elevator opens.

INT. MIDTOWN - BACCHUS'S LAIR - MOMENTS LATER
It's a very elegant room, with spotless furniture and pastel-colored tapestries on the walls. It feels very comfortable, and yet very wrong. There are people all around the room on soft chairs or sofas, trying out some drugs and grinning in

a stupor. At the far end of the room, at a desk, is BACCHUS. He stands up and greets the Squad with open arms.

BACCHUS

Welcome! Welcome, my friends! I've been expecting you!

The Squad look at each other, confused.

BACCHUS

Oh, no need for violence, I assure you. We have much to discuss.

MAX

You're Bacchus?

BACCHUS

Bacchus is only a borrowed name. Philip Walton, at your service.

MAX

Uh...
(still confused)
Surrender peaceably, or we'll open fire.

Bacchus raises his hands in a mock gesture.

BACCHUS

And so I do. However, I need to speak to you most urgently before you take me in.

DOC CEDRICK

He's quite poised for a drug lord.

BACCHUS

All I do is only to help people forget their worries for
a short while.
(gestures to the people)
Everyone here is trying out my latest creation. I call it
"DreamState." Anyone care for a sample? It's on the
house, of course.

Max is about to lose it. This is all too weird.

MAX

Look, buddy. We're an Executioner Squad, and we've
been sent here to capture if not kill you, and you're being nice to us?
(pause)
What the fuck is going on?!

One of the drug-heads walks over to him in a daze and tugs on his sleeve.

DRUG HEAD #1
(whispering)
Hey, man you need to lighten up.

Max clearly looks uncomfortable. The other Squad members start laughing. So
does Bacchus for a bit.

BACCHUS

Hehehe, but anyway...
(gets serious)
I need you all to come with me please. There are
things in motion which demand your immediate
attention.

He turns on a holograph in a corner of the room. Images of mass rioting flash by on the screen.

BACCHUS

This is happening all over the city, if not the country. Police forces have been stretched thin, and even your Executioner comrades have their hands full. It's been like this all day.

MAX

How did this happen?

BACCHUS

GPE has fallen. The handiwork of my former partner, Robert Hessman.

DOC CEDRICK

Hessman? So you know Dr. Pike?

BACCHUS

I worked with Herbert one time before on a top-secret mutation project, code-named Chimara, a former scientist and board member at GPE.

DOC CEDRICK

Then why are you down here selling narcotics?

Bacchus opens a door in the corner.

BACCHUS

A man has to make a living somehow. Besides, you'll probably want to see this.

INT. BACCHUS'S LABORATORY - MOMENTS LATER
Bacchus leads them to his lab, where there are rows and rows of chemicals on display, and charts of profit margins from the past few years. There is a locker on the far side marked with Biohazard logos.

> BACCHUS
> What you really want is right here in this locker.

Bacchus opens the locker and draws out a box containing some small vials.

> DOC CEDRICK
> Is that the cure?

> BACCHUS
> No. They are anti-mutagens. They have nothing to do with the plague.

> DOC CEDRICK
> What? Then why does Hartford need those?

> BACCHUS
> It's not Hartford, your Chief, that wants these. It's Hessman. To destroy them.

> MAX
> What's going on? Why is Hessman suddenly in on all this?

> BACCHUS
> (groaning)
> Alright, here's what I know: when I worked on Project Chimara at GPE, I found an encrypted file amid the various reports.

DOC CEDRICK

Dr. Pike mentioned that he saw something like that as well.

BACCHUS

Perhaps he did. But I cracked the file's code, and found out Hessman's plot. The bankrupting of GPE, the mass panic, it's all tied to him, including the plague! He planned this all from the very beginning.

JILL

What is this, a conspiracy?

BACCHUS

In a matter of speaking, yes.

DOC CEDRICK

How do you know all this?

BACCHUS

I was with the Project since the beginning. I couldn't go on, knowing what it was all about, what Hessman was aiming to do all along.

BISHOP

And that is?

BACCHUS

(gets close to Bishop)

Mutation. On a global scale. Humans, Akaritans, everyone.

Logan scoffs.

LOGAN

What's so bad about that? I'm a mutant. So is Jill.

BACCHUS

That's not the point. He wants to control them all. Some sort of master race, as it were.

DOC CEDRICK

I seem to recall there was a powerful German dictator in the early 20th century who started a war about that.

BACCHUS

This would be worse. Much worse.

DOC CEDRICK

Hmm, and all this coming from a man named after the ancient Roman deity of wine.

BACCHUS

After tonight, I think I'll name myself Apollo, after the god of wisdom. As you may already be aware, this isn't the first time GPE has tried to raise mutants. Several years ago there was a voluntary program. However, thanks to overbreeding, GPE had to round up most of them and kill them. They could not control what they created.

JILL

Ugh.

BACCHUS

Indeed. That's why this time, Hessman is forcing it onto everyone. With everyone out of a job and him being a multi-trillionaire he literally will be able to control the entire economy in the states including the global markets. That makes things even more complicated. With so much chaos and panic, Hessman will be able to force everyone to take his mutant strain all over the earth to be a part of his new order. It will be madness.

MAX

And you waited until now to tell someone?

BACCHUS

I had no choice. I had to go into hiding and disappear after I found out his plans. Hessman has many ties to the government and CIA. Where could I go to get help? I couldn't alert anyone. If I did, I would've been killed.

MAX

What about the plague?

BACCHUS

Also Hessman's creation, but he didn't release it. Someone else did.

BISHOP

Who did?

BACCHUS

Our greatest enemy.

Bacchus goes back to the main entry room, and the Squad follows.

INT. MIDTOWN - BACCHUS'S LAIR - MOMENTS LATER
All of the people that were once drugged out are well-armed and facing the Squad. Bacchus stands proudly.

BACCHUS
Gentlemen and lady present, I give you Phalanx, the
Human Resistance Force.

They can't believe it. They've just been led into the lion's den. Bacchus points
to two high-ranking Phalanx Officers, a man and a woman -- ERICKSON and
MATHESON.

BACCHUS
These are Commanders Erickson and Matheson.
They've been my eyes and ears for a while.

ERICKSON
The rules of the game have changed, Executioners. Law
and order's not worth fighting for anymore. The truth is.

MATHESON
(points to Doc)
Who's the scale-head?

DOC CEDRICK
Dr. Cornelius Cedrick, forensics.

MAX
You want us to work for you, he comes with us.

MATHESON
(a pause)
Alright... just clean up after him. Bad enough to have
two aliens in here.

DOC CEDRICK
I beg your pardon?

Dr. Pike walks among the humans.

DR. PIKE

Cornelius? Is that you?

DOC CEDRICK

Herbert!

They shake hands like old friends.

DOC CEDRICK

So you told Bacchus everything, right?

DR. PIKE

Actually, he contacted me first. When I found out
about what was going on, I fled from GPE. Good
thing I got out in time.

BISHOP

(butting in)

Hey, people. Upstairs. Outside. Place going to hell.
Let's get to work!

Bacchus tries to get down to business.

BACCHUS

As I mentioned before, the plague was created by
Hessman. The one who dispersed it was Zalmon, an
Akaritan terrorist. He's the leader of a international
syndicate bent on killing every human and taking the
Earth entirely for the Akaritans.

ERICKSON

And he's been giving us the business lately. Between
the cops and the plague and now Hessman ripping off
the entire world, Zalmon's not making this any easier.

MAX

I bet.

Max turns around and sits on a couch.

MAX

Weird how you guys are taking Akaritans under your
wing these days.

ERICKSON

A conquering army usually seeks help from the na-
tives, or in our case, a re-conquering army, and...

Erickson sees the implant mark left on the back of his neck.

ERICKSON

...Christ, you've got a tracker?!

MAX

Huh? Yeah, we all do.

ERICKSON

Ugh. Someone get the removal kit over here!

A Phalanx Officer brings out a metal box containing a an electromagnet device
and long tweezers. Erickson holds Max's head down while Matheson zaps his

neck with the magnet and takes tweezers to the wound, pulling out the implant. Max yelps in pain as the device is ripped from his neck.

> MAX
>
> Aaah!

> ERICKSON
>
> Hold still. It'll only be a second.

The device is ripped out, and Max rubs his neck painfully.

> ERICKSON
> (to the others)
>
> Next?

All of the Squad members are grabbed by more Phalanx officers and held down with the faces pointed at the floor.

> MATHESON
>
> Relax, creep squad. This won't kill you, at least not if we do it right.

On cue, all of their implants are yanked out. Logan freaks out a bit; he hates being held down, and he struggles violently.

> LOGAN
>
> Let me go! Yaaaaaahhh!

His implant is pulled out like a tumor. He rubs the back of his neck painfully, scowling.

> MATHESON
>
> Now be a good little doggy, and shut the fuck up!

Logan flips her off with a clawed middle finger.

INT. HARTFORD'S OFFICE - DAY

The phones are ringing off the hook, and outside the office police are in a mad scramble. Hartford gets off his personal phone, and checks his computer, then his tracker device. Five red blips are shown in part of a list. Those five are inactive trackers, and they belonged to the Squad.

HARTFORD
(sighing)
Well, that's one less problem. Goodbye losers.

A cop busts into the office, he looks really out of breath.

POLICE OFFICER
Sir, we're losing a lot of men out there! The National Guard's been called in! It's a warzone out there!

HARTFORD
(grumbles)
Oh really? Where'd you read about that? The book of I already fucking know! Get back to work!

POLICE OFFICER
Hey, what do you want from us? We're getting hammered out there and your lard ass is sitting right here all day!

Hartford growls, and pulls out a gun, cocking it.

HARTFORD
Then suit up! I'm going with you.

INT. POLICE HQ - MOMENTS LATER
Hartford and the cop are moving through the teeming masses of other cops. The sight of Hartford in full gear rallies their spirits a bit, but Amber is among them, and she runs up to her father.

> AMBER HARTFORD
> Dad, don't tell me you're actually going out there.

> HARTFORD
> Amber, I want you to lock yourself in the Archives room. Seal the door and don't open it until I call you, okay?

> AMBER HARTFORD
> Dad! It's really dangerous out there!

> HARTFORD
> Do as I say! You'll be safe in there. Go now, and stay inside!

Hartford leaves, but Amber goes somewhere else other than the Archives.

EXT. MIDTOWN - BACCHUS'S LAIR - DAY
There are mass riots happening right outside in Bacchus's neighborhood. Houses are being broken into and looted. Most if not all of the rioters are human and some mutants. Off to a corner, there is a large contingent of Akaritan militia who are carving a swath right through the rioters. They are heavily armed and mowing down humans without regret.

INT. MIDTOWN - BACCHUS'S LAIR - DAY
Bacchus is watching the news on the holograph while the Squad is ingraining themselves among Phalanx.

MAX

The implants are dead now? Hartford can't find us?

MATHESON

Dead as dirt. You're off the grid now. You don't have to worry about the government or anything now, except staying alive and not causing any problems for us.

Off to a side, Doc and Dr. Pike are talking away from most of the humans. They're still not comfortable.

DOC CEDRICK

So tell me again, Herbert. How did you find out about all this?

DR. PIKE

Well, do you remember File 820? The encrypted file?

DOC CEDRICK

Yes...?

DR. PIKE

Well, Dr. Walton over there helped me decrypt it. He still had some connections to GPE servers, and what we found on there was more or less Hessman's grand design.

DOC CEDRICK

The mutants?

DR. PIKE

He's planning to disperse mutagens on a global scale. Humans and Akaritans everywhere will be affected. Almost like biological warfare.

DOC CEDRICK

Can't be warfare if there's no side to fight back.

Jill butts in.

JILL

No side to fight back? Of course there is: you guys!

DR. PIKE

You're already a mutant. Wouldn't you be affected by any of this?

JILL

Being a mutant, who wants to go through it a second time? And besides, if all the humans are mutated, where do I get blood from? Mutant blood tastes like dog food.

DOC CEDRICK

Um, I'm almost embarrassed to ask, but do you by chance drink from Akaritans as well?

JILL

I did once. The guy screwed me.

DOC CEDRICK

And...?

JILL

Akaritan blood... tastes like glue.

DR. PIKE

Well, I'm sorry to disappoint you.

JILL

Whatever doc. Huh? What's going on over there?

Jill's attention is to the holograph, where the images of rioting are taking a step back to an Akaritan militia onslaught.

JILL

Hey, isn't that Midtown?

DOC CEDRICK

Hmm, it does. Wait... that's not too far from here!

Instantly, the Phalanx forces are mobilizing. Guns are being hoisted and reloaded. Bacchus is in a scramble to lock up some papers and stuff his pockets with backup files. Bishop primes himself for battle.

BACCHUS

You five can sit this one out. I have a contingency set aside for just such a thing.

Onscreen, the violence has reached Bacchus's doorstep, and some alien marauders are busting in. Upstairs, there are sounds of screaming. Bacchus hits a hidden button on his desk.

INT. MIDTOWN - BACCHUS'S LAIR - HALLWAY - DAY
Upstairs, a force field is activated in front of the elevator shaft. A huge shield of energy forms a glowing wall. One alien tries to run headfirst into it, and gets incinerated on contact. Some of the others try to shoot at it with laser weapons and human sidearms, but the lasers and bullets ricochet off the shield and impact against their users.

INT. MIDTOWN - BACCHUS'S LAIR - MOMENTS LATER
Bacchus turns the holograph to his security feed, showing the action from upstairs. Bishop is impressed.

                    BACCHUS
I love science.

                  DOC CEDRICK
Most impressive, Dr. Walton. With inventions like
these, you could have earned a top position at GPE.

                    BACCHUS
I prefer to work alone without corporate politics.

                    ERICKSON
Sir! They're in the halls! The shield can't hold forever!
We've got to evacuate now!

                    BACCHUS
Right. Open the passages and get the anti-mutagens
from my lab. As soon as everyone's out, I'll trigger the
self-destruct.

Erickson scurries to the lab, and everyone else follows him.

                    ERICKSON
This way, people! We're getting out!

As everyone files out of the room and through the lab, Bacchus grabs his briefcase with the anti-mutagens in it as well as a data disc of all his work that is
backed up. He presses another button on his desk, and then runs out of the
place. Alarms sound, which gradually get faster and faster until finally... BOOM!
The place explodes in a burst of fire and shrapnel. In the hallway, the aliens are
incinerated and crushed as the building falls down upon them.

INT. PHALANX TUNNELS - DAY

The Phalanx army and the Squad are moving through some well-lit tunnels lined with metal. They feel a rumble from above, but the tunnels are still safe.

> BISHOP
>
> What was that?

> BACCHUS
> (running up)
> A going-away present to our other guests.

> BISHOP
>
> What guests? You mean us?

> BACCHUS
>
> No. I meant Phalanx's old friend Zalmon. Perhaps you'll get to meet him soon.

EXT. NEW YORK CITY - NIGHT

Hessman and Snyder are riding in a Hovercraft far above the city. Snyder can see huge battles erupting beneath them. The city looks a lot worse than ever. It's hell on earth.

> HESSMAN
>
> Like I said, this is just the beginning.

> SNYDER
>
> After all this? How do you expect to get everything back on track?

HESSMAN

Lawrence, it can only get better from here. And that's
where we come in.

They fly over the city, past the shoreline and over the ocean, leaving the bright
lights of New York far behind them.

EXT. OIL RIG - MILITARY BASE - MOMENTS LATER

Hessman and Snyder arrive at a massive abandoned oil rig out in the ocean. The
decaying, rusty hulk has been converted into a GPE weapons testing facility, so
there is still a satellite uplink to GPE there. They land at a landing bay on top of
the rig, then head downstairs to a control room.

INT. OIL RIG CONTROL ROOM - MOMENTS LATER

The two walk into a small but well-stocked control room. Computer monitors
are showing GPE projects and news, including that their stocks dropped to zero,
and showing a casualty list of everyone lost in the riots. Hessman pulls up a chair
in front of a console, and starts inputting some passwords.

HESSMAN

Good, they didn't revoke my access.

He inputs some data, with Snyder watching.

HESSMAN

Alright, the mutagens were already stocked aboard
the next satellite series that GPE was going to launch.
Hmm, they made it quite easy for us.

More keystrokes, and he relaxes in his seat, as if he just beat a computer
game.

SNYDER

The satellites were launched?

HESSMAN

Countdown is automated. It will take a while for them
to get into orbit and then get linked to us. We'll have
some time to wait.

SNYDER

How long, do you think?

HESSMAN

About a day or so. Is there any food on this rig?

INT. PHALANX HIDEOUT - NIGHT

The Phalanx crew assembles in a large underground room, filled with weapons
and computers. Bacchus gets to his private terminal and looks at some Phalanx
reports while Max tries to talk to him.

MAX

So this is Phalanx, huh? The whole rebel terrorist
group that everyone's so afraid of?

BACCHUS

Not rebels, Max. Just a group of people defending their
homes, or in this case their planet.

MAX

I see. "Humans above all else" and all that, right?

BACCHUS

From the looks of it, you're the only real human from
your squad.

MAX

I was. Everyone else is either a cyborg, alien, werewolf
or vampire, eh, sorry, <u>mutant</u>.

Max flashes a sarcastic look at Jill, who flips him off.

> BACCHUS
>
> Well, at least you've been good enough to hold them all together.

> MAX
>
> I didn't have a choice. They made me leader of the team, it was part of my sentence.

> BACCHUS
> (at computer)
>
> At least here you can put your skills to better use than serving a broken-down police state.

He taps at his screen to patch into a news feed.

> BACCHUS
>
> Ah, I see Zalmon is making his move. Care to watch?

Onscreen is an Akaritan warlord, ZALMON, in a fancy military outfit, flanked by Akaritan guards.

> ZALMON
> (speaking Akaritan language, translated)
>
> The fall of Global Placement Enterprises is clinching proof that humans are incompetent and primitive, unable to control even their own endeavors! Rise up, sons of Akarai! Let us drive these parasites called humans to their graves and take the Earth for our own! Let this human culture of waste, abuse and exploitation be forever wiped away and forgotten! And the meager forces of Phalanx

will be made example of! Humans have never deserved the Earth, let it be taken from them! <u>Tamath makal!</u>

AKARITAN SOLDIERS
(in unison)

<u>Tamath makal!</u>

Bacchus turns off the screen. Everyone gives each other looks.

JILL

"Tamath Makal?"

DOC CEDRICK

It's an Akaritan phrase. Essentially it means "our world."

ERICKSON

And he's the guy responsible for half of everything that's wrong with the city. You know the plague?

DOC CEDRICK

Yes?

ERICKSON

He released it in the form of a hormone street drug. Mine are different. I created Dream State to combat the plague. Hopefully, be able to cure it one day.

JILL

You knew about that all along? Why didn't you people say anything? They've been trying to figure out where it came from for a year!

ERICKSON

Sorry kid. We had to take care of ourselves. And we couldn't just go in front of the press out in the open.

BACCHUS

It's unfortunate, but it couldn't be risked. We could've lost everything by going public.

BISHOP

It's a bit late for saying what you could've done. What the hell are we going to do right now?

MATHESON

The riots are still going on above us, and Zalmon's forces are on the move. We can't get out. We're trapped.

BACCHUS

But every moment we spend down here gives Hessman more time to make his move.
(turns to Dr. Pike)
Herbert, can you patch into GPE's system from here?

DR. PIKE

I can. Give me some room.

Dr. Pike takes over at the computer terminal, logging in to GPE and looking over their files.

BACCHUS

Perhaps we could see what R&D has been doing recently.

DR. PIKE

Alright. Hmm... just some casualty lists, loss of funds, hmmm... here's something. There have been a series of satellite launches just an hour ago.

BACCHUS

Satellites?

DR. PIKE

Yes. Remotely fired. They were carrying... by the gods! They have Ed9X!

DOC CEDRICK

Mutagens.

DR. PIKE

Probably in an aerosol form that he can disperse in the atmosphere.

MAX

Great. As if starting an economic collapse isn't enough, now he's going to have us all breathing in poison.

BACCHUS

Can you shut them down from here?

DR. PIKE

I can't. Hessman probably has the satellite uplink codes. We'll need him for that. Sorry Executioners, looks like we'll need him alive.

Max grumbles.

BACCHUS

Where is he? Find any recent signals that could have activated those satellites?

DR. PIKE

I'm looking! Don't rush me!
                    (delves further)
All of GPE's signals have gone dark since the crash. All of them...
                    (points to a map onscreen)
Except this one.

DR. PIKE

There's an abandoned oil rig about fifteen miles off the coast. The company used it for weapons testing. It's the only active GPE signal around.

DOC CEDRICK

And that's where Hessman would be?

DR. PIKE

Most likely.

MAX

So we go over there, bomb the place and pull Hessman out of the ruins?

DR. PIKE

Like I said, they used it for weapons tests. It won't be easy. It's basically a fortress on water.

BISHOP

Then we'll need a lot of firepower to break through
their defenses.

JILL

And wouldn't you know it? You guys have a pilot on
our side!

BACCHUS

Phalanx does have some aircraft left over, and plenty
of weapons.

LOGAN

Now you're talking!

INT. PHALANX TUNNELS - MOMENTS LATER

A Phalanx guard is patrolling the tunnels. He seems something moving in the
shadows, something not human. He raises his weapon.

PHALANX HUMAN #1

Who's there?

He gets shredded with laser fire from offscreen. Dies. Several Akaritan militia
enter, with Zalmon at their side.

ZALMON

This must be the place. Get the rubble upstairs cleared
away to make way for the others.

AKARITAN SOLDIERS

Sir, perhaps we can drill through?

ZALMON

Hmm, perfect. You two, drill down to the contact's
position. The rest of you, clear a path through the ruins
for reinforcements to move! <u>Now!</u>

INT. PHALANX HIDEOUT - NIGHT

They all heard some noises through the tunnels. Max looks uneasy.

MAX

Another going-away present, Bacchus?

BACCHUS

No, I already triggered the self-destruct. That sounded
closer... from the tunnels!

MAX

Someone's in here with us! We gotta get out, now!

ERICKSON
(to soldiers)
You guys! Arm weapons and follow me! If something's
in the tunnels, we'll flush them out!

Erickson takes a squad with him. As soon as they leave the room, there is an
explosion and some of them scatter and go flying in the blast. The others in the
room shield their eyes. From out of the smoldering crater comes a few Akaritan
soldiers and Zalmon himself!

BACCHUS

<u>Zalmon!</u> You son of a bitch!

Zalmon looks around, admiring Phalanx's work.

ZALMON

Hmm, human technology. Amateur, but still practical.
<u>Kill them!</u>

Matheson runs out in front of Zalmon, unarmed.

MATHESON

Wait! That wasn't the deal!

BACCHUS

Matheson, you traitor!

MATHESON

You owe me for this, Zalmon! Ten million credits!

Zalmon shoots her.

ZALMON

Money... is a human construct. I've no need of it, or you.
(turns to the others)
<u>Tamath makal!</u>

There is a firefight. Bacchus and the other Squad members run for cover, then as
soon as they find some weapons, they return fire. Human and Akaritan bodies
start to pile up as some Phalanx Officers have some limbs and heads blasted off.
Zalmon's forces are also suffering casualties, as their viscous, dark-blue/green
blood starts oozing from gaping wounds. The Squad is held up behind some
heavily damaged cabinets and computer mainframes.

MAX

(growling)

Is there any way out?!

BACCHUS
East tunnel! It leads out to the streets!

Bishop dodges fire, and shoots back.

BISHOP
Can't take much more of this!

Jill and Logan are still fighting back. Doc and Dr. Pike are on the ground, trying to protect themselves. Bishop heaves a grenade over their cover point.

BISHOP
<u>Fire in the hole!</u>

An explosion rips apart Zalmon's forces. Right after that, Bacchus, Max, Bishop, Jill, Logan, Doc and Dr. Pike make their escape. Zalmon is on the ground, wounded but still alive. He heals himself and some of his comrades.

ZALMON
After them! Don't let those humans get away!

INT. PHALANX TUNNELS - MOMENTS LATER
The Squad and Bacchus and Dr. Pike run through the tunnels, picking off Akaritan soldiers behind them. They run through the twisting, narrow, barely-lit corridors until they reach a metal door. Bishop rips it open and they all run out into the night.

EXT. SLUMS - MOMENTS LATER
The Squad emerges from a well-hidden door in a slum, and outside there is a riot in full swing. The Rioters are all armed. The Squad shoots their way through the Rioters and heads down the street. Zalmon also comes out from the tunnel, but he and his soldiers are held up among the crowd. They weren't expecting resistance like this.

During the firefight, Max is aiming his weapon at rioters, and he bumps back-to-back with Hartford, who is at a command post with some cops.

HARTFORD
You?! What the hell are you doing here?!

MAX
No time to explain! Behind you!

Max shoots a rioter that was gunning for Hartford. Hartford can't believe it.

HARTFORD
You saved me!

MAX
Hey, I'm a cop.

The fight continues, and Zalmon is getting closer. Jill and Logan are ripping throats out, and Bishop is blasting Rioters and even punching through some torsos with his cybernetic enhancements. Doc and Dr. Pike are holed up in a small house, with Doc shooting at some Rioters in the windows.

Along the way, most of the Rioters are dispersing, but Hartford took some shots to the torso. He falls near Max, who has to hold him. Doc and Dr. Pike emerge from their hiding spot, and the others walk over to him. Zalmon is getting closer.

HARTFORD
Agh...
(in pain)
Oh, God...!

MAX
Chief?

HARTFORD

No... I'm done... Watch Amber for me. I'm sorry... I was the guy who set you all up.

MAX

I know.

HARTFORD

You guys... are good cops. I was the bad guy. <u>Hess... man!</u>

Hartford dies. Max doesn't know how to take this; he may have been an asshole, but at least he admitted it. And he mentioned Hessman!

Behind them, Zalmon is standing right there, hearing everything. His soldiers are poised to attack. Max lays down Hartford's body and reaches for a weapon. The others are getting ready to make a stand.

ZALMON

...Stand down! Let them go.

The mood is tense. There's a standoff with the Squad and Bacchus against an alien terrorist leader who made it clear that he hates humanity. Zalmon takes a step forward.

ZALMON

This man... he was your ally?

MAX

Yes.

ZALMON

And you allowed him to die?

MAX

I tried to save him.

A beat.

ZALMON

Hmmm... interesting. A human sentiment.

BACCHUS
(stepping forward)
Zalmon, as representative of Phalanx, I'd like to offer
a truce.

Zalmon looks at him.

BACCHUS

We know that there is a man, a half-breed, who is planning to destroy both our races. He wants to turn humans and Akaritans into a new species, something he
controls.

Zalmon doesn't want to believe this. His soldiers are still aiming guns at
them.

BACCHUS

We have a common enemy. If we cannot fight this,
then we all lose everything. There won't be any victory
for Akaritans, or anyone else.

ZALMON

...What are you saying, half-breed?

DOC CEDRICK

A man named Robert Hessman, former vice-head of
GPE, will disperse mutagens around the world, and all
species will be affected, even us.
(gestures to himself and Zalmon)
Humans may be frail and oftentimes even inept...

Max looks offended.

DOC CEDRICK

...but their capacity for decency cannot be ignored.
They are capable of love and honor, as well as
Akaritans. We are no different than they are. Hessman
would take away all of that and turn us into something
else, something... without honor.

Zalmon looks around at the Squad, at Bacchus, at Doc, and to his own
soldiers.

ZALMON

All the same it could be a ruse, a human trick... prove
me wrong.

Jill and Logan step in.

LOGAN

We weren't always like this. I was once just a normal
guy, and I got changed.

JILL

I've always been a mutant. I can't ever fit in with regular people. I can't have a normal life. I have to drink
blood, fucking <u>blood</u>, to survive!

Zalmon winces. He's grossed out.

> DOC CEDRICK
>
> And this is what is in store for all of us, even you and me, if we don't act quickly. Hessman will transform and even control us all!

> ZALMON
>
> Not even with a will of our own?

> DOC CEDRICK
>
> Especially not even with a will of our own.

A pause, then Zalmon nods in agreement.

> ZALMON
>
> Then I agree.

Zalmon shakes hands with Doc, and with Max.

> ZALMON
>
> If this Hessman does intend to turn humans and my own people into a new species, then the sons of Akarai will destroy this threat!

EXT. POLICE HQ - MOMENTS LATER

The rioting has moved to different areas, or some pockets of riots were already quelled. The bodies of humans and aliens litter the streets. The combined force of the Squad, Phalanx and Zalmon's army march to the Police Station.

INT. POLICE HQ LANDING BAY - MOMENTS LATER

The combined force takes some fighter jets and two personnel transports for their troops. In a repeat of past events, Amber taps Max on the shoulder, and Max still flinches.

MAX

Aagh! Amber! I told you not to do that!

AMBER HARTFORD

I've been here all along. I was just about to take a jet into the air myself when I saw the riots moving too close.

MAX

Amber... your father's dead.

Amber looks shocked, almost ready to cry. Max puts a hand on her shoulder.

MAX

Listen, you have to be strong right now. I know it hurts, but we need to focus. There's a suspect who caused all of this, and we need to take him down. Can you get us all clear to take off?

Amber draws a deep breath.

AMBER HARTFORD

Yes... and I'm going with you!

MAX

(sighs)

Fine. You'll be flying with Jill. She's a pro. Stay with her.

JILL

Right.

EXT. POLICE HQ - BREAK ROOM - MOMENTS LATER
The jets and carriers are taking off, streaking out of the back of the building and into the night. The moonlight bathes the ocean in a ghostly silver light as they fly far away from the city.

INT. AERIAL APC - NIGHT
Jill is flying with Amber in the backseat.

> MAX
>
> Okay, Dr. Pike. How do you think we should handle this?

> DR. PIKE
>
> Well, I did learn that the facility is well-defended. They used to have offshore raiders try to steal tech from there. There may be some gun turrets lining the main platforms, so we'll need to disable those before making an incursion on the rig.

> JILL
> (over the comm)
>
> I'll take care of that.

> DR. PIKE
>
> Good. Okay, and after that, it's possible he may have other defenses as well. How much in the way of weaponry do we have?

> BISHOP
>
> All the Phalanx guys we came with, and we still have some extra guns onboard.

LOGAN

Didn't Zalmon bring some new toys as well?

DOC CEDRICK

I believe he did. Courtesy of our old friend Abaddon.

LOGAN

You gotta be kidding me! He <u>did</u> have real weapons?!

DOC CEDRICK

Pretty much. I assume Abaddon was simply being, how
you put it, a "cheapskate" to some of his clients.

Everyone laughs a bit. Bacchus grabs one of the handrails, and his comm is ringing.

BACCHUS

Bacchus here.

ZALMON (V.O.)

You are the half-human, yes?

BACCHUS

I am. Being part Akaritan is interesting, to say the least.

ZALMON (V.O.)

Perhaps. The sons of Akarai will be under my command, but it will be in our interest to work with your
human comrades on this mission.

LOGAN

(sarcastically)

And what about the mutants? Isn't anyone going to say
hi to us?

ZALMON

Whatever it may take to prevent us all from becoming monstrous creatures.

LOGAN

Fuck you!

A beat.

ZALMON (V.O.)

...We will cover the southern platform on the facility once the defenses are down. You may land on the other side and we can prevent the Hess-man from escaping.

MAX

Good idea. Zalmon can take his guys on that side, maybe take them to the lower levels so Hessman can't get to a lifeboat. The Phalanx team can take the top level and cover the helipads. And us...
(to Bishop, Logan, Jill and Doc)
That leaves us with a straight shot down the middle, right into the belly of the beast.

BISHOP

Okay, Jonah.

DOC CEDRICK

Jonah?

BISHOP

It's a long story. Whatever.

                              JILL
              We're almost there, guys! Strap in!

INT. OIL RIG CONTROL ROOM - MOMENTS LATER
Hessman and Snyder are looking at a monitor which shows several inbound aircraft coming right at them. Hessman operates the controls of the defense grid.

                            HESSMAN
              Hmm, looks like we have visitors.

                            SNYDER
              Pulse cannons or missiles?

                            HESSMAN
              Both! Take them down, now!

EXT. OIL RIG - MILITARY BASE - MOMENTS LATER
A series of cannons and missile launchers come online and open fire, turning
the sky into a raging inferno of missiles and streams of machine gun bullets. The
heat-seeking missiles streak through the air and explode two fighters.

INT. AERIAL APC - MOMENTS LATER

                              MAX
              Evasive action! We got heat-seekers!

Jill pulls the carrier into a huge upward thrust to avoid some fire. Everyone
inside is thrown against a wall as the carrier lifts higher and higher, and bullets
ricochet against the armor plating.

EXT. OIL RIG - MILITARY BASE - MOMENTS LATER
The sky is filled with chaos as the remaining fighters make passes at the oil rig's defense systems. Some of the fighters have sustained damage, and they fly with plumes of dense smoke trailing behind them as they fire missiles and other guns at the rig-based turrets.

INT. AERIAL APC - MOMENTS LATER

JILL

Fuckin' A!

Two heat-seekers are on her tail! She pulls the carrier into a tight spin, still climbing, then back down swiftly, dive-bombing one of the gun turrets. She dodges the hailstorm of fire from the turret, leading the missiles downwards. She pulls up sharply, and the missiles, since they can't bank well, end up detonating right on the gun turret. It explodes.

INT. OIL RIG CONTROL ROOM - MOMENTS LATER
Hessman doesn't like what he sees on the monitors. Most of the gun turrets are down.

HESSMAN

Deploy the drone fighters!

Snyder presses some buttons on the console, and a squadron of small, very thin and maneuverable fighters start to erupt from a shaft on the side of the rig. These fighters, while being very small, are numerous and their mini-missiles and lasers can pack a punch in large numbers. One more fighter is taken down as they swarm all over it.

INT. ZALMON'S AERIAL APC - MOMENTS LATER
Zalmon and his Akaritans are ready to fight back. Zalmon opens the back
hatch of the carrier. Winds are whipping all around him, and he mounts a large
Akaritan cannon to the side of the hatch. He blows away several enemy fighters
with pinpoint precision.

INT. AERIAL APC - MOMENTS LATER
Jill flies over Zalmon's ship, noticing how he's taking the fight to the drones.

JILL

Check out what Zalmon's doing!

LOGAN

Wait... we can do that?

Logan opens the hatch and grabs a rifle almost as big as Zalmon's. He stands
there on the edge of the open hatch and starts blasting the drones gleefully.

LOGAN
(laughing maniacally)

<u>I love my job!</u>

The drones are dropping like flies, and the tide is turning in favor of the Squad.
It's now safe to land on the rig and confront Hessman.

MAX

Right, looks like the defenses are down. Zalmon, you
ready to make your landing?

ZALMON (V.O.)

Affirmative.

MAX

Okay. I saw a lower platform near the ocean, on the north side. Take that area so he can't escape by sea.

ZALMON (V.O.)

Humans can travel on water?

AMBER HARTFORD
(overhearing)

You got a lot to learn, pal.

ZALMON (V.O.)

Perhaps. Prepare for ground combat.

MAX

Phalanx guys?

ERICKSON (V.O.)

Copy.

MAX

Take the high platform on the south side. If there are any other aircraft there, destroy them. Can't let Hessman get out that way either.

ERICKSON (V.O.)

Roger that.

Max turns off his comm and looks around in the cabin. Bishop looks up at him, as does Logan and Doc. Bacchus looks outside a window and Jill and Amber are steadying the carrier to land on a nearby platform between the north and south areas.

MAX

Guys, it's been an honor serving with you. Now let's go kick some ass!

LOGAN

Thank you for flying Death Squad Airlines. Please return your seats and tray tables to their upright and locked position and shit.

JILL

I'm supposed to say that, you furball!

They land on a platform underneath the main helipad and pile out of the carrier, all of them fully armed and ready for battle. Max leads them in a tight formation into the rig's interior.

INT. OIL RIG HALLWAYS - MOMENTS LATER

The Squad moves in through the narrow metal hallways. Dr. Pike and Bacchus are in the back, with Max taking point. They look all around, pointing weapons in every direction. They round a corner, and suddenly BOOM! They are under fire from the far end of the hall! Max gets behind the corner and fires blind, then the shooting stops. They round the corner to investigate, and they find a human with an animalistic face. He was wearing armor with holes punched through it.

BISHOP

The hell is that?

DOC CEDRICK

A mutant. There might be more of them around here.

JILL

Hey Logan, he almost looks like you!

LOGAN

Shut up.

An alarm blares throughout the rig, and the Squad makes a run for it into the nearest unlocked room. It's a mess hall.

INT. OIL RING MESS HALL - MOMENTS LATER

The squad takes cover behind some counters and tables as a horde of armed mutants swarm into the room. A firefight ensues. Max and Bishop are pinned down behind a table closest to their line of fire. They return fire as much as they can, but their enemies are not going down easily. Logan and Jill are fighting back, but Jill is running out of ammo. Doc and Bacchus and Dr. Pike are shooting rather wildly, hardly hitting anything.

MAX

Can't take much more of this!

Jill gets up from her cover position and throws a handful of three grenades right over her comrades' heads and into the mutant horde.

JILL

<u>Hit the deck!</u>

They all take cover as a large explosion engulfs the side of the room. Most of the mutants are incinerated. The rest of them are too badly wounded to fight on. They can be picked off easily.

MAX

(catching his breath)

Everyone alright?

BISHOP

Yeah. Let's move, people!

Thankfully, nobody has wounded, but Dr. Pike is plenty shaken from the battle.

INT. OIL RIG CONTROL ROOM - MOMENTS LATER
Hessman is furious that the Squad broke through his defenses.

> HESSMAN
> They're getting through!

> SNYDER
> Robert, what are going to do now?

> HESSMAN
> What you're going to do is man the hell up or I'll kill you myself! Just keep the doors locked. Satellites are almost in range.

While Hessman is working with the satellites, Snyder pulls a snub-nosed gun from his pocket and points it at Hessman.

> HESSMAN
> <u>What the hell?</u>

> SNYDER
> You didn't pay me enough for this shit!

Before Snyder can shoot, Hessman twists his arm around and breaks it. Hessman grabs the gun and shoots him in the thighs.

> SNYDER
> (screams)
> Aaaaah! You son of a bitch! Aaahhh!

HESSMAN

I'll at least let you see the beginning of the new age. It
will be the last thing you ever see, my friend.

The satellites are now in position on the monitor. Hessman taps in some codes,
when the door flies open and the Squad pours into the room.

MAX

Freeze, Hessman! It's over!

HESSMAN

Not yet!

Hessman has his finger over a button on the console. Snyder is on the floor, still
in pain. He grabs the gun from the floor and aims wildly. He winds up shooting
Max in the neck. Max dies, and Logan instinctively leaps on Snyder and feasts
upon him, ripping him to pieces with his teeth and claws, eating him alive as he
screams his last.
    Hessman is distracted, but retreats to the console.

HESSMAN

Back off, all of you! All I have to do is press one button
and transmit my code to the satellites, and then all of
you will be changed! Nothing can stop the dawn of the
new order, where everyone is the same, all the same
species!

Jill opens fire and the console explodes in a burst of sparks.

JILL

Okay, what button?

Amid the flames and the ruins of the console, Hessman looks ready to have a mental breakdown. He falls to his knees and screams.

HESSMAN

<u>No!!!</u> My dream... Everything I've ever worked for --

BISHOP

(interrupting)

-- is over.

HESSMAN

I only wanted to make the world a better place! I only wanted to save the human race... and the Akaritans... from themselves!

DOC CEDRICK

To force a change upon all free-thinkers will improve nothing.

BISHOP

Robert Hessman... you're under arrest.

EXT. NEW YORK CITY - NIGHT

The survivors of the attack fly in formation above the city. Bacchus and Zalmon are in a carrier together, looking at each other with accomplished looks. In the squad's own carrier, Hessman is being kept under very tight guard. They fly over to the police station.

INT. POLICE STATION LANDING BAY - MOMENTS LATER

They touch down at the landing bay, and Amber and the squad escort Hessman in for processing.

INT. POLICE HQ - INTERROGATION ROOM - MOMENTS LATER
Hessman gets socked by Bishop's mechanical arm. Jill and Logan are also present, and they're all really pissed off.

BISHOP
That one's for Max! And <u>this</u> one is for everyone else!

Bishop socks him harder, then pulls out a knife, cutting him twice on his left arm. Then he takes a can of salt and pours it on the wounds. The white salt mixes with the blood, and Hessman shrieks in pain.

BISHOP
You thought you must've been really clever, don't you? Try to release a bunch of toxins to mutate everyone on Earth, and cover your tracks by ripping off your own company? Huh? You think that was clever?

HESSMAN
Ugh... you can have the money...

Bishop cuts and salts another wound. Hessman screams again.

BISHOP
We're not taking the money, you're going to give it back to those you stole it from!

Jill lustfully licks some salted blood from Hessman's arm.

JILL
Mmmm, salty.

HESSMAN

Ugh... erh... crazy bitch!

BISHOP

Where's the money, Hessman? All of it!

HESSMAN

(catching his breath)

Offshore accounts... you'll never find it!

Bishop salts another wound, and Hessman screams again.

HESSMAN

Alright, alright, I'll give you the accounts, all of them, just let me go!

BISHOP

(withdrawing knife)

Alright. There's a recorder in this room. Say everything to that.

INT. POLICE HQ - ANTECHAMBER - MOMENTS LATER

Doc, Dr. Pike and Amber are watching the scene unfold.

DOC CEDRICK

Barbaric. But fitting.

AMBER HARTFORD

Usually, this would get an officer suspended, but he deserves it, and besides, I guess I'm in charge now, as the new commissioner.

DR. PIKE

Mankind and the Akaritan race... we could have lost our identities.

DOC CEDRICK

And what about Bacchus and Zalmon?

AMBER HARTFORD

I released them, under the condition that they never return to the States again, and stay out of trouble. I think this whole thing might've left a mark on them.

DOC CEDRICK

Perhaps.

Amber has a ringing comm device that she answers.

AMBER HARTFORD

Commissioner Amber Hartford here.

A beat as she listens to the comm.

AMBER HARTFORD

Yes sir. It will be done.

She hangs up.

AMBER HARTFORD

That was the governor. He's passing down a sentence of execution for Hessman.

She looks at Hessman in the interrogation room, still talking to the recorder about his offshore accounts and how to access them.

> AMBER HARTFORD
> And I think I know just the way to do it. But first things first.

INT. ARCHIVES ROOM - MOMENTS LATER

At the large supercomputer in the Archives room, Amber hacks into each of Hessman's accounts and re-wires the money back into GPE's stock holdings, then sends reports to the press that a technical error led to the stock fluctuating, but the money is returned (and there's even enough left over to transfer to several anti-poverty charities, too). She also sends a video log of Hessman in the interrogation room, which gets transmitted to every screen in New York City, including Times Square and local and national news channels.

> HESSMAN (V.O.)
> (onscreen)
> There's nothing left to say. My entire goal was to mutate the entire population of Earth into a new master race. And I covered my tracks by bankrupting GPE, stealing all of their funds and keeping it in secret accounts. I had no regard for the damage it would cause, only seeing the dream realized, and now it's over. I have nothing left to live for. So go ahead and kill me. I deserve it.

EXT. NEW YORK CITY - MOMENTS LATER

A single carrier flies over the city, with a chain dangling from its underside. Hessman, bruised and beaten, is tied up and dangling like a worm on a hook above the angry mobs in the streets. Many of them were directly affected by the financial crash and the riots that followed, and they're out for some justice.

The chain lowers, and Hessman is lowered right into the mob. He knows his time is coming, but he never expected it to be anything like this.

> HESSMAN
> No! Don't do this! I didn't mean it! Any of it! I -- I can pay you all! Just let me go!

> RIOTER
> Too late, asshole! We got our money back! Time to die!

Hessman is lowered into the mob and gets torn to pieces. The carrier flies away, and Jill is at the helm.

INT. GPE - BOARDROOM - EVENING

An hour later at GPE Headquarters, a press conference is being held with GPE commenting on the chaos caused by Hessman and the heroic exploits of the Executioner Squad Program barraged by reporters and flashing cameras documenting this historic event. GPE spokesman, LARRY THOMPSON, 30's, speaks at the podium. A poised man. Sharp as a tack. Professional as can be.

> MR. THOMPSON
> Ladies and gentlemen. It's GPE's deepest regret that our fair city and nation was held captive to the caprices of a narcissistic and corrupted member of this corporation. We have received news that Robert Hessman has been executed by the state. Justice has been served and the victims are satisfied, as are we. GPE will be offering full restitution to all of our stockholders and to the general public. A restoration project is in the works at this very moment to rebuild the destroyed parts of New York and recovery funds are being worked on with Washington, DC

at this very moment to repair that damage that was caused to this great nation and all of our people both Akaritan,

MR. THOMPHSON

Mutant and Human alike. To get the public back to work, GPE will be offering work programs to help aid all citizens of New York and all around the United States. Advancement we believe in and so we shall advance and bring back the financial standing and great pride of our home and country. Above all we like to thank New York's finest including the Executioner Program. We honor these brave men and woman for their service: Max Prescott who lost his life today for our city and his country. And those who survived -- Jill Morgan, Logan Kennedy, Bishop Cain and Doctor Corneilus Cedrick. We thank you. As for the Phalanx Organization in their co opera- tion to take down Hessman, they have been given a full pardon by the state and have been made new of- ficers in the ISRA program. Thank you all for your support.

The crowd cheers for the victory of the people.
TV SCREEN SNOW APPEARS AND CUTS THE FEED.

EXT. CEMETERY - MORNING
The bodies of Max Prescott and Joseph Hartford are laid to rest at a grand po- lice funeral procession. Hundreds of Officers in full dress uniform, including the surviving Squad members Bishop, Jill, Logan and Doc, are in attendance. Dr. Pike is there as well among the mourners. A moment of silence is given a the crowd stands over hearing the Catholic Priest speak before the lowering of the coffins.

CATHOLIC PRIEST

We gather here this day to lay rest to the lives of Max William Prescott and Joseph J. Hartford. Two police officers who gave their lives in fighting for the freedom of this city during all chaos that has happened. Please bow your heads as we pray.

The crowd is silent and they bow in silence to reflect.

CATHOLIC PRIEST

Heavenly Father, we come before you to commit their bodies to ground to lay in the earth until the new resurrection comes. Ashes to ashes. Dust to dust. Let their souls and valor live forever as they may brought to eternal life through your son, our Lord, Jesus Christ.

The coffins are lowered in the ground with commemorative music played with a 21-gun salute with a human and Akaritan and mutant squad.

After the funeral ends the crowd disperses to leave the cemetery. Amber walks up to Logan and Bishop to talk.

AMBER HARTFORD
(talking to the Squad)

Guys, you all did great. And the Board's deciding to relieve you from your duty. Your sentences are done.

LOGAN

And all it took was one little disaster to make it happen.

AMBER HARTFORD
(giggles)

Yeah, anyway, you guys can have your lives back. You can go home, get normal jobs.

BISHOP

I can go back to my family?

Amber nods.

LOGAN

Sweet deal, but I don't know what to do now. The fighting circuits are long gone for me.

JILL

Being a pilot is my life. It's in my blood. I think I'll stick around.

LOGAN

Same here.

BISHOP

Sure, why the hell not? We've all spilled the same blood together.

AMBER HARTFORD

In that case, I can promote all of you to honorary NYPD captains, with jurisdiction over different areas of the city. How about it?

BISHOP

Sounds good. I miss being a hero.

LOGAN

I'm in.

JILL

Cool.

AMBER HARTFORD

Good. You know, the city is throwing a black-tie event
for the police force, and you guys are welcome to come.

LOGAN

I love to party.

INT. THE ATHANAEUM HOTEL - EVENING

There is a massive ballroom, where police Officers and their spouses are danc-
ing, dining and drinking. Bishop and his wife are on the dance floor, all dressed
in fancy dresses and suits and ties. Bishop's wife holds him close as they dance.
Dr. Pike and Doc Cedrick are among them as well, dressed in tuxes talking with
the mayor and city officials while enjoying some cocktails. Logan is dressed in a
black suit and tie, standing off to a side looking rather uncomfortable. Jill walks
up to him, wearing a stunning red dress.

JILL

Not having fun?

LOGAN

I'm not used to parties like this. Too rich-blood for me.

JILL
(flirting)

I have a better idea.

She whispers something in Logan's ear, and he perks up.

LOGAN

Oh...hell yeah!

(beat)

New York. Baby, what a town.

As the jazz music plays in the background, the camera pulls away to show the New York City skyline, which looks much better than it used to in the beginning. No fires, no gunshots, not as many police choppers. A ray of hope for a new future to begin...

THE END

www.ingramcontent.com/pod-product-compliance
Lightning Source LLC
Chambersburg PA
CBHW071251130626
46556CB00003B/1258